Cave

Of

Secrets

Hal Burton

Cave of Secrets

Copyright © 2002 by Hal Burton

All right reserved. No part of this book may be used or reproduced without permission of the copyright owner.

All characters in this book are fictitious, and any resemblance to actual persons, living or dead, is purely coincidental.

Printed and Bound by Gorham Printing
   Rochester, Washington

Published by Hal Burton Publishing
   Lilliwaup, Washington

First Edition, First Printing

Cover by Jeanette Burton and Nora Haugan

Junk depictions from Chinese woodblock print

ISBN   0-9725707-0-5
Library of Congress Control Number: 20002094682

Cave

Of

Secrets

Hal Burton

To my family and friends who gave me the the encouragement to write this story.

Special thanks to my son Greg Burton for his editorial skill and story line suggestions, to Jay Shelledy for his editorial inputs and to my wife Jeanette for her publishing assistance, story line suggestions and unwavering support.

Cave of Secrets

Who They Are
499 AD

Lin Ming-na -------- Chinese crewman
Chu Hin-qua -------- Chinese crewman
Chung wa-Loo ------ Convoy captain
Hwui Shan ---------- Buddhist monk
Chiang Pao-Tse ---- Buddhist monk
Tetacus & Manaloc- Makah Indians
Kuneki -------------- Makah Indian girl
Lakslii --------------- Makah Indian girl
Kalapoo ------------- Lakslii's mother

1966 AD

Jerry Helspath -------Teenager – Boy Scout
Bill Jenkins ---------- Jerry's friend
Kay Helspath ------- Jerry's sister
Dave Peterson ---   Friend of Jerry & Bill

1981 AD

Chuck Coolridge -- History Professor
Karen Black -------- Chuck's girlfriend
Wen Hao-tung ------ Chinese research assistant
Wang Chin-tsi   Minister Peoples Republic
Lu Xun -----------   Intelligence Agent – PRC
Woo Xinghai -----   Senior US Agent – PRC
Miles Varney ------ Captain, S S Monrovia
John Yang   ----   Consul – Taiwan Consulate
Maria Lee -----   University professor
Jason Winslow ---- Reporter
Brian Hill ----------- Graduate student
Will Grove --------- Makah Ranger
Esther Grove -----   Will Grove's mother
Ben Maxwell ------- County Sheriff
Jerry Helspath ----- Forest Ranger
Bill Jenkins ---------- Mill Worker

Cave of Secrets

Prologue

The Olympic Coast on the northwest corner of the state of Washington remains one of the most remote areas in the western United States. This is especially true north of Grays Harbor County where US Highway 101 turns inland and most of the coastal region along the shores of the Pacific is accessible only by old logging roads and hiking trails.

The Olympic National Forest and National Park cover the peninsula and most of the ocean beaches north of the mouth of the Hoh River are within Park boundaries.

Nine Indian Tribes inhabited the peninsula 1500 to 2000 years ago. Their ancestors still do today. Some live on the reservations that dot the region. Many are active Native American businessmen and leaders in their communities. Others assimilated into the mix of Europeans that explored and settled on the peninsula from early in the 16th century until modern times.

The Makah, Quileute, Copalis, Quinault and Hoh tribes dominated the northwest coast. One of the main Makah villages was near Lake Ozette, south of Cape Flattery.

Landslides from heavy rains and ocean pounding shape the coastline today as they have for centuries. Moving land erodes the rocks and new shapes emerge. Caves and tunnels lurk everywhere. Some wide-open and visible one year and sealed the next by moving rock and mud. A catastrophic landslide 500 hundred years ago buried much of the Makah village near Ozette. Archaeologists worked at the site until 1981 when it was abandoned for lack of federal funds and back-filled to protect the site from looters.

At the same time early Native American cultures were developing, a continent away Chinese cultural development was experiencing one of its greatest eras. Missionary trips by Buddhist monks spread their culture and religion throughout the ancient world.

It is speculated, though never proven, that the first explorers to the coastal region of Washington were monks from China. Several accounts have been found in Chinese court records that tell of missionary trips to the Aleutian Islands and as far south as Baja California.

One such account chronicles the voyage of a convoy of three ocean-going junks that set out from northern China in 499 AD. Little was known of their fate until a history professor from the University of Washington found ancient ship logs and the court records of their journey.

魏 Chapter One

499 AD

The large white gull swooped down, plucked the small fish and flew to a nearby rock to eat his meal. He is one of thousands of gulls of several varieties that make the rocky ocean coast its home. Some gulls prey on other coastal birds, stealing their eggs from nests on the rocky cliffs. Others feast on the crustaceans and mollusks exposed at low tide. Here the weather is mild year round. The region is warmed in the winter by currents from the west and protected in the summer from the heat further inland by a range of mountains to the east.

More than a millenium later, when men from another continent would claim discovery of this land, they would marvel at its raw beauty and watch in awe the power of the ocean surf as it blasts against the huge rocks that dot the coast line.

This season the storms have been unusually severe and the battle between sea and rock was no contest. If man attempted to fight these forces of nature, he usually lost. The late afternoon sky was clear, but in the distance, out over the white capped waves, another storm was mounting.

In a few hours, the sun would set on the fifth day since the seamen had set up camp on the beach in this strange land. Chu Hin-qua and Lin Ming-na began to realize their worst fears. Unless they had misread the crude map or missed some of the signs left during their journey two weeks ago, the two junks from the Chinese convoy were either very late or they themselves were at the wrong place.

In the tenth month of year, darkness came early and with it, the cold and dampness.

"Sit closer to the fire, Hin-qua."

He nodded and added a few more sticks of driftwood to the small fire. Ming-na was preparing to cook what was left of the days catch. It had stormed that morning and their makeshift shelter of logs and branches needed repairs.

Ming-na's injured shoulder had been slow to heal, so Hin-qua did most of the repair work. Both were ready for sleep soon after eating. The sun accommodated them and quickly dropped behind the large cone shaped rock 30 yards off shore.

"Maybe they'll come tomorrow", Ming-na said to Hing-qua as he drifted off to sleep.

"Yes, I hope so," as he too let sleep overcome thoughts of what they would do if the junks did not return.

Four years earlier Ming-na had just finished his third trip of his second season aboard his uncle's fishing boat. It had been a poor season. The normally abundant tuna schools were farther out to sea where the risks of late summer storms increased. In fact, they had lost one of the five crewmen last week and had to turn back with only a half-filled hold. His uncle, Lin Tse-hsu asked Ming-na to assist in finding a replacement for the next sailing. The third person they talked to was Hin-qua.

At fifteen he was a year younger than Ming-na and the age when the young men of the village sought life at sea to escape the drudgery of sheep herding for the landowners of the region. Ming-na remembered Hin-qua from his days working for landowner Chao.

Hin-qua seemed not to recognize him, however. And no wonder. He now stood at five feet six and life at sea had filled out his once thin frame. His face and arms were darker and his cue was wrapped in the style of an adult.

"Want to trade the smell of sheep dung for tuna guts, huh?" Hin-qua frowned, then slowly broke into a grin. "Ming-na!"

So it was that the two friends sailed the next week on his uncle's boat. Their village of Hsinking was up river from the port city of Laichow. As they rounded the jetty and headed for the open sea, Ming-na told Hin-qua of his wish to one-day sail on the ocean going junks anchored in the harbor.

Ocean going junks were now regularly going on trading missions to the Japan's. It was said that the Buddhists monks, eager to spread their influence, were backing the voyages.

The next spring, Ming-na's wish came true. Both he and Hin-qua sought to be on the crew of the Shangti, but only he was accepted. Hin-qua would have to wait another year, but Ming-na's uncle, impressed with his work the previous year, gladly accepted his nephew's friend back on his tuna boat crew.

The Shangti was small for an ocean going junk, having only 10 sails and a crew of 400. The captain, Mao Dun, was known for his seamanship, especially navigation, and the Shangti was regularly chartered even though larger junks could carry more cargo. It seemed huge to Ming-na when compared to his uncle's boat.

The large main sails were square in shape and attached to crossbars hung at the center of each mast. The panels of the sails appeared to be of cloth and were held flat by thin strips of some material. He learned later that these were made of bamboo. The bow jutted up at a sharp angle, but it was the stern that was massive, seemingly twice the distance from the water line as the bow. And the rudder! Ming-na had steered his uncle's boat, but it looked like it would take 10 men to keep this ship on course.

As one of the new crew, Ming-na was assigned to the cookhouse.

The voyage to the Japan's took 8 days. During this time, Ming-na had few chances to improve his seamanship.

On the return trip, one of the senior men instructed him and several others in the art of sailing an ocean going Junk. By the end of the journey, he was able to follow the commands for pulling the ropes to spread or close the sails. There were four crossbars on each of the masts, so it took a large crew to operate the ship under full sail.

During the following winter months the news spread fast through the village that the monks from Laichow were planning a major trading expedition in the spring. Hundreds of crewmen would be needed. Ming-na heard of the expedition through his friends that had crewed with him on the Shangti. They were told that the Shangti would be one of the ships in a convoy of three.

As the weeks past, even more was learned. The expedition would last at least a year and it was said they were going to a land very far away. Also that the two other junks were coming from the major port of Cheefoo, would provision in

Cave of Secrets

Laichow, and then sail with the Shangti to the city of Changchun to pick up more cargo. Ming-na was convinced that this would be Hin-qua's chance to join him on the Shangti.

Spring arrived and Ming-na learned that the expedition was to be headed by the famous monk Hwui Shan and they would be leaving in one month. The other two junks were larger than the Shangti, with 12 sails, instead of 10, and a crew of 500 each.

One junk, the Changtsi, would be captained by the famous leader, Chung wa-Loo. He would be the senior captain for the voyage. The captains of the Shangti and the other junk would report to Captain Chung.

Captain Mao Dun of the Shangti asked all of his crew to go, but several of the married men declined due to the length of the voyage.

The pay was to be substantial though, 4 Zhu, so the captain of the Shangti had little trouble recruiting new men. Hin-qua was one of these. What a sight it was when the three junks in full sail left Laichow and headed north to Changchun.

Ming-na was now a regular on one of the 5 crews that handled the rigging. Like his friend before him, as a new crewman, Hin-qua was assigned to the cookhouse. He would likely be reassigned to one of the rigging crews, for like his friend, he had filled out. Almost as tall as Ming-na, his physic showed the results of two years on a fishing boat. There was no doubt he could pull his own weight.

They reached Changchun in three days. Here, the other two junks took on a few supplies, but the Shangti sat at anchor without any activity. Then on their second day in the harbor, two large launches were oared to the Shangti.

As the launches approached, Ming-na noticed that the lead one contained many Buddhist monks. The two dozen or so monks climbed the ropes awkwardly in their long, flowing robes. Several of the observing crewmen snickered, but were hurriedly quieted by the crew leaders. Ming-na and four others were ordered to assist in loading the cargo from the second launch. It consisted of three large crates, each very heavy, and one smaller crate. The latter was quickly removed from it's sling and carried aft by two of the monks. The heavier crates were stowed below in the stern of the junk. Within an hour they were under sail.

Ming-na new little of navigation and couldn't read anyway, but from what his uncle had taught him, he believed they were heading south. Then on the seventh day he recognized some landmarks that told him they were nearing the Japan's.

Here, however, the course seemed to turn northward which was confirmed in a few days when the air turned much cooler. During the next week, he had a chance to see Hin-qua several times. They constantly speculated about their destination and the adventure that lay ahead.

As the weather turned bitter cold and two storms tossed the Shangti about till it seemed she would split into, the days grew less enjoyable and their romanticism faded.

Finally the weather improved and there was reported sightings of land as they headed first westerly and then south. They continued south for two days. All the while it seemed like they were sailing in a narrow channel surrounded on both sides by mounds of ice.

As the channel widened, the ice was less frequent. The days became warmer. Then when Ming-na thought he would never see trees again, he awoke one morning to find they had entered a large harbor framed in the tallest trees he had ever seen.

The convoy dropped anchor and several small boats from the Changtsi, the junk carrying Captain Chung, went ashore. Hin-qua joined Ming-na at the rail."Have you ever seen so many trees, and so tall, too?" Ming-na shook his head, but was silent. *I wonder where we are,* he thought.

Shortly the lead men announced to their crews that they would be here for several days to provision and do repairs. On the second day at anchor, Ming-na and 15 men went ashore in two boats. A monk went along in each boat. They were cautioned to be on guard, as the group from the Changtsi reported seeing some people with long hair and in strange dress. These strangers, assumed to be natives, did not approach, but seemed content to observe from afar.

Ming-na's group never saw any of the natives, but did manage to kill two deer and return with five casks of fresh water.

When they returned one of the crewman from the other boat that had gone ashore told Ming-na that they had encountered two of the natives and that the monk tried to communicate with them. Ming-na never heard any more about the strange natives and two days later they pulled anchor and headed south once again.

The wind was calm at first and they made minimal headway. Then on the second day the wind picked up and Ming-na noticed some dark clouds in the distance.

****

The storm hit the convoy with a savage fury just as they left the land Hwui Shan had named Tai Wei. He chose the name to honor his mentor, the Taoist monk Wei Ne. The junk Shangti floundered on the rocks and broke apart on the shore. A few of the crew, like Ming-na and Hin-qua, jumped overboard before the Shangti hit the rocks and were picked up by the junk Changtsi. The rest were presumed dead in the wreckage or drowned. The larger two junks were heavily damaged and put into shore for repairs at the mouth of a small river a two days sail south of Tai Wei. In the senior captain Chung's estimation, most of the wreckage of the Shangti lay about a five-day journey north by land. He also estimated it would take about a week to repair the surviving junks and set sail, presuming that local materials could be used to repair the plaited bamboo sails on both junks.

Hwui Shan agreed to a plan to send 16 sixteen crewmen north by land to the wreckage, recover the chests and what ever else of value could be salvaged and await the two junks return. Hwui Shan's nephew, Chiang Pao-Tse would lead the expedition. A good plan all agreed. Hopefully, any natives Chiang and his crew would encounter would be as friendly as the ones from the land of Tai Wei.

The monks had finally decided that the name the people of Tai Wei called themselves sounded like "Mah-kaa" and that's what Hwui Shan had recorded in his journal. Either way, the Buddhist monks insisted, and Hwui Shan as their leader agreed, the chests must be found. No risk was too great. After all, it had been his decision to put them on the Shangti instead of one of the other larger junks. Without those chests their voyage was doomed.

****

The expedition was ill fated.

Hin-qua and Ming-na were the only two of the expedition that survived the five-day trip north along the rugged coastline. The rest of the sixteen and their leader, Chiang Pao-Tse, had been killed just a day ago.

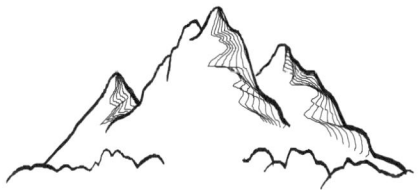

Chapter Two

1966 AD

The Chehalis River flows into the Pacific Ocean at Grays Harbor on the Washington coast. The principal cities fronting the harbor are Aberdeen and Hoquiam where forest products are the dominant source of income. Westport, at the southern end of the harbor, is a busy commercial and sport fishing town. To the north, Ocean Shores is more of a residential resort. The shoreline is dotted with motels offering weekend get-aways. Aberdeen was the childhood home of Jerry Helspath and Bill Jenkins.

Jerry and Bill had been close friends since grade school. Both loved the outdoors and spent as much time together fishing, hiking and exploring the Olympic Peninsula, as their parents allowed. In high school, when most boys have long since turned their interests in other directions, Bill and Jerry stayed in the Boy Scouts. Besides their interest in the outdoors, they also shared a passion for Stamp Collecting. But in summer, mountains and rivers won out over little pieces of paper. Both were counselors at Camp Parsons in the summers.

Cave of Secrets

Camp Parsons was on Hood Canal on the eastside of the peninsula. After four years at Parsons, each had led other scouts on many hiking trips through the Olympic Mountains and along the coastal trails. Jerry's Scout leader the first two years at Parsons had just completed his training to be a Forest Ranger, and Jerry was convinced that's what he wanted to do after college. He planned to major in Forestry.

Jerry was several inches taller than Bill, standing six feet by the time he was fourteen. His brown hair was perpetually in a crew cut.

Bill had bright red hair and was typically freckle faced. Like Jerry, his hair was close-cropped. Bill was an only child, but Jerry had a younger sister named Kay. Bill treated Kay like his kid sister, which lately seemed to irritate her.

During the camp session of 1966, Dave Peterson from Seattle was Jerry's section assistant in the Ranger section. Over the summer he, Jerry and Bill became close friends.

One of Jerry and Bill's favorite hikes in the Olympic National Park was from the Rialto Beach to Lake Ozette. The summer of 1966, before Jerry left for college in eastern Washington and Bill started working at the mill in Forks, it was only natural that they planned this hike as their last.

Bill was fairly certain he wouldn't be drafted. A football injury to his spleen in his sophomore year had taken care of that. Jerry would be deferred till after he graduated from college, but everyone figured the war in Vietnam would be over by then anyway. The hike looked like a sure thing.

They planned the trip out during the evening hours in Jerry and Dave's cabin. Dave began to get as excited as Bill and Jerry. He told them that he had been to Ozette last Spring and knew the area a little. So, in the end, they invited Dave to join them. They decided to leave two days after the last session at Camp Parsons.

The hike from Rialto to Ozette required a driver to leave and pick them up. They asked Kay, who had just gotten her license. So she drove them to the Rialto Beach parking area on Sunday and promised to pick them up at the parking area near Cape Alava the following Saturday. Kay had just finished her summer camp session at Camp Robbinswold, the Girl Scout camp on Hood Canal, and had already driven several hours that day.

She was tired but happy to help her brother and pleased to be able to spend time with Bill.

"Have fun and be careful," said Kay waving goodbye.

"Watch out for the high tides. You wouldn't want to get your rear ends wet," she added with a sassy laugh.

"We will Sis. You just be sure you're at Ozette on time," Jerry said turning back to face his sister.

Bill, who was beginning to look at Jerry's kid sister differently, silently wished she were coming along. She was now sixteen. The way she filled out her jeans and tee shirt was evidence that she was not the gangly girl of a few summers ago.

"See you Kay," he called after her. He still wished she was coming.

"Did you say something Bill?" she asked. She turned back to face him and as she did, her sun bleached ponytail flipped about. She giggled as it brushed her face.

"Nothing," he said sheepishly. Dave thought to say something to kid Bill, but thought better of it. Kay smiled and started to respond, but she could see her brother was getting impatient. She just smiled again and waved goodbye.

"Let's go guys, we have four hours and I want to be at Cape

Cave of Secrets

Johnson before dark."

It was a clear, brisk day on the beach. Jerry took the lead and Bill quickly picked up his pace. Dave hesitated a moment to tighten his pack straps, then followed. He was excited about being with his new friends and anxious to show them his knowledge of the coastal area.

"Hey, wait up you guys," he called to Jerry and Bill as they rounded a large pile of driftwood. A gull swooped down looking for a handout and seemed to call to them as they headed north on their adventure. Another landed on a log then quickly took flight as Dave hurried by.

****

1981 AD

Chuck Coolridge had one year left to complete his doctorate at the University of Washington in Seattle. His field of study was Chinese History, especially the early dynasties. His dissertation was to be on Explorations by Chinese to the North American Continent during the Chin and Wei dynasties, between 300-600 AD.

His research focused on the voyages supposedly made to the West Coast, although never verified, specifically those near the Washington Coast.

Chuck had returned to the University in 1971 to get his Master's degree through the GI Bill. Poor eyesight kept him out of combat and Vietnam during his Air Force tour. The results of his physical at San Antonio's Lackland Air Force Base, after graduation in 1966, ruined his plans to be a pilot. He got through Navigator school at Ellington Air Force Base, in Houston, but his eyesight worsened. He spent the remainder of his four years as an electronics instructor at Kessler Air Force Base in Mississippi.

When he finished his tour, he got a job with an electronics component manufacturer in Cleveland, Ohio, but after two years he was ready to return to his native Seattle. He applied and was accepted into graduate school in the History department. During the three years he took three courses on ancient Chinese history taught by Professor Ed Bailey. He soon found that Asian history, especially Chinese, was his passion. Professor Bailey helped him get a teaching position at the University after receiving his Masters.

Unlike many of his colleagues at the University in the 70's, Chuck kept his hair at collar length, wore a tie and jacket when teaching and was not vocal about the war. He did grow a beard, which he kept neatly trimmed. His girl friend, Karen Black, told him it made him seem taller and more distinguished. He shaved off the beard when he received the grant to do research for his dissertation in Taiwan. Professor Bailey told him that the Chinese thought it more proper to be clean-shaven.

Chuck was scheduled to leave for Taiwan on June 15. In the two months prior to departure he focused all his efforts on improving his skill at reading the ancient Chinese scripts, especially Kai-shu, which would be a must in his research.

Chuck spent most of the summer of 1981 at the National Palace Museum in Taipei searching the archives for information on western explorations in the 4th through 7th

centuries. Most of the history of that period was recorded in court records. Just about all of these had been brought to Taiwan in 1949 when Chiang Kai-skek and his followers retreated from the mainland. As part of his study grant, Chuck had been assigned an assistant curator, Wen Hao-tung, to help him with the translations and interpretations. The translations made it slow going and by early August he only had a few weeks to go before he had to return to Seattle. To date they had looked primarily in the records from the Southern Dynasties.

"Here are the court records from the Northern Wei dynasty and some from the latter part of the Chin era. We might as well start on these today," said Hao-tung, eager to please.

"And, Chuck, I've put a page marker in the third volume covering the years from 480 to 500 AD. I seem to remember that's when the Buddhists in the north were backing exploration. It was also during this time in the north that the shipbuilding would have advanced enough to support making large, ocean-going junks."

The large, cloth bound books were heavy and awkward to handle. The protective latex gloves he and Hao-tung wore made it even more difficult. Chuck set the book down and adjusted his glasses. Even with interpretive help from Hao-tung, the small script was hard to read.

"Thanks Hao-tung, lets get started. This old Kai-shu script doesn't get any easier," Chuck said, tracing his finger over the ancient rice paper.

Kai-shu script had been used from about 380 AD to the present but since about 1300 AD the form has simplified. The script from the 5th and 6th centuries is harder to read. Some of the script they had just finished seemed to be a mix of the ancient Li-shu script and the more recent Kai-shu.

That night in his room at the Taipei Grand Hotel, Chuck thought about the day's efforts. Again, he wished he had had more time to study Kai-shu script before he left Seattle. He finished the Taiwan Ale he had gotten from the cooler in his room, marked the room concession list and got ready for bed. Tomorrows another day, he thought.

****

At the same time, 1200 miles away, in the city of Beijing, Arts and Antiquities Minister Wang Chin-tsi listened to a briefing by intelligence agent Lu Xun on the progress of Chuck Coolridge's research in Taiwan.

"He has not found anything substantial yet," Lu related in a polite but confident tone.

Lu Xun was a career intelligence officer with a good rank, but the Minister's quick temper and rancor were well known. Lu was nervous and cautious of his words.

"Maybe you should not depend so much on Kai-hui's abilities," Minister Wang warned.

"No, I think she is close enough to Hao-tung that he would tell her about his day to day work with Coolridge," Lu responded, not quite so confident as before.

"Finding those chests, especially the sacred urn, and returning them to their rightful place is most important," said Wang. "Is this clear?"

Wang continued as if delivering a speech. "At the same time, it is important that we not open ourselves up to problems with Americans. We have just started our new 10 year Plan and good relations with them is key to attracting western technology."

"Yes it is clear Minister, but our agents overseas may not be able to get to them before someone else does. Assuming they're even found?" Lu said.

Sensing the minister's irritation Lu added, "You know that Coolridge may not even recognize what he discovers, even if he does find references to Hwui Shan's voyage and the holy urn."

"Yes, I realize, and I know it's a long shot, but we must be prepared to act if Coolridge is successful. Keep me informed," said Wang with a nod, signifying that the meeting was over.

****

A year earlier, some workers excavating for a new building in the northern city of Changchun had uncovered the opening to a huge hillside cavern. The walls of the cavern were covered with paintings and writings. There were several large sculptures showing junks seemingly being prepared for departure. As Wang was minister of Arts and Antiquities, he was contacted by the local officials and with a small staff traveled to Changchun to inspect the find.

After several months of research they determined that the depictions and sculptures told of the impending voyage of a monk named Hwui Shan, in the year 499 AD. The Buddhists from the north were active in explorations in the Pacific Ocean in the latter part of the 5th century. It wasn't surprising to find such evidence. Further research showed that Hwui Shan planned to follow the Pacific rim northward from China past Kamchatka, across the Aleutians and eventually southward to what is now called Mexico.

Here, it was conjectured, he would establish Buddhism, build temples and form trade alliances with the natives. What really got minister Wang's attention was the wall writing near the largest sculpture and the sculpture itself.

It clearly slowed the loading of huge chests onto the smallest of the three junks, the Shangti, and the ancient script told that the chests were filled with gold Zhu coins.

But the most shocking and significant revelation was what was in a fourth chest. It was said to contain an urn with the ashes of the great Buddha Gautama.

After establishing the monastic order of Sangha, Buddha Gautama died at age 80 at Kusinagara about 483 BC. His corpse was cremated and eight urns with his ashes were divided among his devotes and then buried under large mounds called stupas.

But the cave sculptures and wall paintings detailed an urn with Buddha Gautama's ashes being placed in a chest and loaded on the Shangti in 499 AD. How could this be?

Minister Wang speculated that the monk Hwui Shan had some how acquired one of the eight urns and planned to use it as part of his missionary work in the New World. Perhaps it had been secreted by the Sangha monastic order and not buried like the other urns. Or maybe there was another explanation: that there originally were nine urns rather than eight and the existence of the ninth urn had been kept secret for almost 1000 years!

Weeks of further research though found no additional records to explain what happened to the convoy of three junks, the monk Hwui Shan, and, more importantly, the gold coinage and the chest containing the urn. The value of the gold, as interpreted from the writings, would be worth over 40 million dollars today, not counting the intrinsic value of the coins. The urn, if found and authentic, would be valuable beyond words. A nice present for Chairman Mao's treasury and a feather in Wang's cap should he be able to find and return the treasure. Something finally of great value that Chiang and his bandits had not stolen away to Formosa in 1949.

Unfortunately, most of the records that might reveal the fate of the convoy were on the island of Formosa and in possession of the Nationalists at their Palace Museum.

Wang knew the government had spies on Formosa who might help, but it seemed he was at a dead end. That is, until early June of 1981.

A senior intelligence agent Lu Xun, had reported through channels that one of his female agents in Formosa, a Wong Kai-hui, had knowledge that an American, one Chuck Coolridge, received permission to do research on Chinese voyages to the western part of the United States in the early part of the millennium. His aide was to be an assistant curator named Wen Hao-tung. As luck would have it, Hao-tung's current girl friend was none other than agent Wong Kai-hui.

魏Chapter Three

499 AD

The monk Hwui Shan and captain Chung had made no headway north. The storm that had battered Hin-qua and Ming-na's shelter that morning had forced the two vessels further south from the safe harbor where they had finished repairs two days before.

The monk turned to Captain Chung as they stood together on the forward deck.

"Captain, you know the value of the contents of those chests when we reach the southern lands."

"Yes, but we don't even know whether your nephew, Pao-Tse, and his men found the wreckage," Chung responded.

Hwui Shan gave a sigh and turned to go below. Then reflecting on their earlier conversation, he hesitated.

"Pao-Tse is my nephew, as you said. Besides the loss of the chests, it pains me to leave him in this unforsaken land."

Chung nodded. "I know, but for today we must put back into shore for shelter."

"Maybe tomorrow we can try again by sea or consider sending another group by land," Hwui Shan persisted against the Captain's doubtful tone. Chung didn't answer. He knew they were too far south to consider another land expedition.

Cave of Secrets

****

Several miles north on the beach, the two surviving crewmen awoke early. A decision was made. One of them would go back to make sure the three chests they found were still secure in the cave. And at what cost? Fifteen dead and now it looked like they were going to be stranded in this foreign land. Pao-Tse had taken a calculated risk that day but it had all gone wrong. Ming-na decided he should go.

As he retraced their steps back to the rock outcropping to check on the condition of the cave approach, Ming-na thought about that fateful day.

Though they had found the wreckage mostly intact, there were no survivors. What human remains were still on the beach were being hastily consumed by the crabs and seagulls. Three of the four chests were located, two large and one small. The chests appeared to be in good condition. That first night they camped on the beach using fallen trees as shelter.

The next day a scout from their party reported seeing some natives on the ridge above. Pao-Tse decided that it would be wise to hide the chests just in case the natives weren't friendly. He calculated they had a couple of days left before the junks would pick them up. Dividing into three teams, they scouted the beach and cliffs above for several miles north and south for a secure hiding spot, perhaps one large enough for the groups' shelter if another storm came along. Their present shelter would not weather another storm.

The terrain rising above the beach was thick with large trees and ground cover. The Chinese had never seen spruce, hemlock and giant red cedars. Most of the tree trunks were densely covered with moss and lichens.

Just to the north, one of the teams found the opening to a large cave about a hundred 100 feet inland behind some large rocks, just above an outcropping part way up a high bluff. The opening was said to be about 30 feet above the beach and it looked easily reachable.

Hin-qua stood post at their beach camp in case the junks returned. Ming-na and the others hoisted the chests and headed for the approach to the cliff.

Ming-na later told Hin-qua that the climb up the cliff was hard going with the heavy chests, but they eventually carried all three into the cave. He was posted just outside the cave opening under the outcropping.

It was then that the hillside gave way, sealing the group inside. All but Ming-na were buried in the slide. Afterwards, there was no sound other than the wind and the rain beating down on the hillside. Ming-na's shoulder ached where one large rock had grazed him. To his horror he saw that the cave entrance was sealed. He would need some help. So he tended to his wounds, left some rock markers and made his way down the cliff and back to the camp where he related the events to Hin-qua. Both seamen were devastated and by nightfall the enormity of their situation was clear.

In the morning, they returned to the cliff. A small opening had been left at the cave's entrance but there were no signs of life and no hope of getting into the cave without some help. They returned to camp to await the return of the convoy. The chests were safe for now. With more help, they could uncover the cave entrance.

"What if the ships do not return?" Hin-qua asked, on the way back to their beach campsite.

Cave of Secrets

"We must assume that they will," answered Ming-na with assurance. Privately he was not so sure. He had just about decided they were on their own in this strange land of big trees, large rocks and the ever-present wind and rain.

****

1966 AD

Jerry, Bill and Dave made good time their first day, and as planned, camped near Cape Johnson that evening. It had been an easy hike except they had forgotten to check the tide charts. The water was a lot farther in than expected. So with no trail over the top of Cape Johnson, they got their boots wet. Bill also got his pants soaked when he stepped into an unseen hole. It reminded them that their tide chart would be a valuable tool. There were several other spots that could only be accessed at low tide.

"Looks like Kay was right," Bill said as he turned the branch holding his pants to expose the other side to the fire.

"What do you mean?" said Jerry. Then he remembered his sister's admonition and smiled.

"The water wasn't exactly up to our rears, but mighty close," Bill chuckled. Dave agreed with Bill, as he had gotten his boots wet too in a hole covered by the high tide. Dave also had slipped on some kelp and skinned his knee.

"Thanks." Dave closed the First Aid kit and handed it back to Jerry.

"No problem. Glad it wasn't worse."

Jerry returned the First Aid kit to his pack and started

rolling out his sleeping bag. It had been a long day.

****

As they broke camp Monday, the rain, a common morning companion along the Washington coastline, started to fall. They donned their rain gear and set out for their next overnight spot, the Norwegian Memorial. Along the way, they intended to explore some of the small coves for unusual shaped driftwood and what ever came in with yesterday's high tide. On a previous trip, Bill and Jerry noticed several caves up high on the banks. Time and tide allowing, they planned to explore some of those.

Most of the large rocks along their route were still several yards off shore, but some were accessible at low tide. Dave slipped behind one large barnacle covered rock near the next bluff while Bill took off his pack to investigate what appeared to be a small cove. Jerry waited with Bill, who crawled through a space between two rocks in front of the cove. "See anything back in there?" asked Jerry.

"Nothing interesting. Maybe a few pieces of dry wood for our fire tonight," Bill answered.

He passed several pieces out. Then hesitating, "Is Dave there with you?"

"No," said Jerry. "He walked ahead toward that next large rock."

"I think he needed some privacy." Then he added, "It must have been those beans we had last night."

Bill crawled back out of the rock opening. "He shouldn't wander off. He doesn't know this beach like we do and the tides coming in."

Carrying their few pieces of wood, Bill and Jerry walked around the next large rock but didn't see Dave. After another five minutes of searching they started to get really concerned. They searched ahead for five minutes then backtracked to the first large bluff where Jerry had last seen Dave. There was no sign of him. They started hollering. They were doubly concerned as the tide was coming in faster then they had planned.

Actually, Dave *had* gone around the bluff as Jerry had remembered. He found a good spot to relieve himself and then decided to hike a little further. Before him was a stretch of large rocks and then a high bank which seemed to rise about 80 feet.

Spindly Fir trees jutted out among the rocks in every direction. He walked around the rocks on the beach up to the base of the bank.

Directly above him, maybe 30 feet up, there appeared to be an opening. *One of those caves Jerry and Bill were talking about*, he thought. *Maybe I'll take a look and surprise them with a discovery*

Dave knew it was not good to get too separated from the other guys, but curiosity and his desire to find something before his pals over rode his normal caution. He started up the bank.

The first 20 feet or so was easy going, although some small rocks and dirt fell on him from above as he climbed and several small hemlock branches and large ferns obscured his view.

In a few minutes he could see the opening and a narrow ledge just in front. It looked like the storm last week had eroded some of the dirt that must have covered the opening for some time. Shortly, Dave reached a rock just to the right of the opening. Grabbing a clump of branches from a nearby hemlock tree, he lowered himself unto the ledge and peered inside. He unhooked his flashlight but the beam didn't illuminate much from his position. Then he saw what he thought were skeletons. What! Maybe his eyes were just playing tricks on him. Should he venture in now or wait for Jerry and Bill?

****

1981 AD

The hours limped by for Chuck Coolridge. It didn't help that his allergies were aggravated by the dust in the museum records room where they worked, sometimes 10 to 12 hours a day. And his back ached as he daily tried to fit his 6-foot frame into the small chairs.

"It seems like no one has been into these old court records in a long time," he said to Hao-tung, yanking out his handkerchief in time for a loud sneeze.

"Yes, it would appear so," Hao-tung answered as he continued reading the entries from a large volume of records. He made a mental note to come early tomorrow and dust the storage area where these books were kept.

On this, the second day of their reading of the court records, they had gotten to the year 499 AD.

And then finally, there it was. "Look here," Hao-tung said loudly, carrying the large volume to where Chuck sat.

Cave of Secrets

"It says here that the monk Hwui Shan left on a missionary trip in 499 AD with three ships and crews of over 1,500 men. At least I think that it was 499, by comparing the modern calendar to the dates in this old script."

"My God, how big were the ships?" responded Chuck so excited he almost dropped the volume he had been reading.

"Each Junk was four decked, was powered by 12 sails and usually had a crew of 400 to 500. Although on this voyage one of the junks, the Shangti, was slightly smaller and likely only had 10 sails and a smaller crew," Hao-tung continued.

"Now here's the exciting part for you, Chuck. Their route was to take them northward to Alaska and down your West Coast. If I read this right, they even planned to go as far as southern Mexico."

Chuck recovered his composure and started reading along with Hao-tung. The next section contained a cargo list from the Shangti, but some of the script characters were difficult to interpret. Hao-tung said they were like abbreviations. He indicated that it would take some time, but he was sure he could make sense out of the notations. He was invaluable to Coolridge and a welcome partner in his research. At 31 years, he was typical of many of the young bureaucrats in Taiwan: close-cut jet-black hair, unmarried, dressed in a dark business suit, educated in America, eager to please and fiercely loyal to the Chiang government.

The two men spent several minutes translating the characters. The lighting was very poor.

Chuck had rigged up some extra desk lamps. The light was better, but still very dim and reading was difficult.

Most of the list was routine food supplies and maintenance items but near the end there were four special notations.

"What does this mean?" asked Chuck pointing to two groups of characters.

Hao-tung seemed puzzled. He studied them for a minute.

"Well, this one certainly stands for a Buddha, but which one, I don't know for sure."

"This is the word for gold and this one is the character for money or coin."

"Isn't this the symbol for *zhu?*" asked Chuck.

"Yes," answered Hao-tung, "which leads me to believe this is an inventory of gold zhu coins. See here, this is the value sign for the number 5."

"So, are you saying this is an inventory of gold zhu coins, each with a value of five?"

Hao-tung went on to explain that during that dynasty a five-zhu coin was minted. However, he had never heard that there were any minted in gold. He doubted they were pure gold. Most likely they were a mixture of gold and silver.

"What are these symbols?" Chuck asked following down the list a little further.

"These characters relate to some type of boxes or chests. These other characters will take some more study."

****

Wen Hao-tung's apartment building in Taipei was on Hsuchow Road. Near the large Chinese Handicraft Mart, a big tourist attraction.

He'd had his apartment for about a year since his promotion at the Museum. Lately he had been sharing his accommodations with Kai-hui.

"I'm exhausted, that was really nice," Hao-tung said with a sigh, reaching over to caress her neck. He marveled at the

the smoothness of her naked body.

"Yes," Kai-hui purred, "Very good".

As a lover, Kai-hui was the best in some time. He was quite fond of her and although promiscuity was frowned on in Taiwan, Hao-tung had risked his position at the Museum to carry on the affair.

They had met at a dinner party for low level bureaucrats. He had been invited to attend by his supervisor at the Museum and was quite taken with her at first glance. He saw her again a few days later near the Chiang Kai-shek Memorial Hall and then a week later at another dinner party in the company of an army captain. He found a moment when she was alone and asked her to dinner the following weekend.

The relationship had gone on now for more than three months and included a three day weekend at Sun Moon Lake. He was in love. Hao-tung hoped Kai-hui wasn't still seeing other men, but she had insatiable appetites and liked expensive presents, so he was constantly in fear of losing her. She was beautiful. Her hair was cut short in the latest western style and perfectly framed her light, almost white skin.

She leaned over and gently kissed him. "Are you tired, my love?"

He returned her kiss and moved his mouth to nibble at her ear lobes. Then his hands began to caress her. She sighed and moved her body closer.

Afterwards they usually talked of their day's activities. Kai-hui worked at the Sun Yat-sen Memorial Hall and although he encouraged her to tell him more about her job, he usually did most of the talking.

"Today Mr. Coolridge and I found records of a voyage to the western part of America. He was excited, almost giddy.

Mr. Coolridge thinks it's just what he needs for his study area at the university."

"That's very interesting. What was the voyage's purpose, does it say?" asked Kai-hui quietly trying not to show any special interest.

He explained that they were not sure but that the court record indicated a large cargo including gold coins and possibly some statues in several large chests.

"What's most interesting is that the voyage seems to have been under the control of Buddhist monks. Their leader was a monk named Hwui Shan."

"What was the date of the voyage?"

"As best we can tell about 500 AD, but until we decipher some more of the old characters we don't know for sure if they reached there destination and if they returned."

****

Chuck arrived early the next morning and found Hao-tung cleaning and dusting the storage area.

"Thanks, I really appreciate this," he said. Then without delay, Chuck pored himself into the rest of the volume. By the time Hao-tung finished his house keeping Chuck was near the end. "Look at this!" Chuck tried not to yell, "I think I've found what we've been looking for!"

Hao-tung stopped his cleaning and joined Chuck. Then, a smile slowly came on his face and he nodded his head in agreement.

****

Cave of Secrets

    Hao-tung related these latest discoveries to his mistress later that night. She tried not to show too much interest, but Kai-hui knew that this new information was important. She would contact agent Lu first thing in the morning.

Hal Burton

499 AD

They called themselves 'Kwih-dich-chuh-ahtx' or People Who Live By the Rocks and Seagulls. They were the natives that one of the Chinese crewmen spotted several days earlier. They lived in the most northwestern point of what would one day be the contiguous United States. Rock carvings told their history dating back to the beginnings of time. These were the people who watched Chiang Pao-Tse and his men struggle up the steep hill with their heavy loads, saw the landslide and for the past several days watched Hin-qua and Ming-na.

They had come ashore with the rest of the eight-man whaling canoe crew to wait out the storm. This third storm in three weeks had battered the coast, devastated the two Chinese crewmen's shelter and either spoiled or scattered their remaining food supply.

Eventually, the skies cleared and two of the Indians, one called Tetacus, and the other Manaloc, decided to investigate the strange men.

"Careful, Tetacus."

Manaloc held back but Tetacus ventured closer, seeing no sign of movement.

Then, to show he too was unafraid, Manaloc also moved to within a few feet of the two inert figures.

"Perhaps they are dead," said Manaloc.

"They may be, but let us see," Tetacus said.

Just then one of the men moaned. With that, Manaloc stopped, but Tetacus continued until he was standing next to the one who had moaned. As it turned out, the two Chinese were near death.

Though leery of the strangers, their natural concerns overwhelmed their fears. They bundled Ming-na and Hin-qua in some whale skin blankets and tried to get them to drink some water. But, Manaloc and Tetacus soon realized they would have to get them back to their village where better care could be provided.

Although the canoe was 32 feet long, there was little extra room. Tetacus and Manaloc made a makeshift sled of split driftwood logs, wrapped Hing-qua and Ming-na into the sled and set out on foot. The rest embarked by sea in the canoe and headed north to their village near the big Lake they called "*Ozette*".

****

Several days later, when the two junks made land fall near the prearranged spot, no one was found. There were scattered signs of the wreckage and evidence of human remains, but no sign of the Pao-Tse party and definitely no chests with coins or the urn.

"Hwui Shan, we have no choice but to return. If we wait too long, the ice will stop us from making it home. Without the gold we have lost our trading power in the southern world. Even if we continue south, we have lost valuable time."

Hwui Shan pondered their choices.

"Let us search again tomorrow. To abandon the urn if it is still to be found would be a great tragedy, but I agree, if we have no success we must return."

Chapter Four

499 AD

Of the two crewmen carried back to the Ozette village, Chu Hin-qua was in the poorest shape. Lack of food, exposure and the injuries sustained in the last storm weakened his condition for the eleven-mile sled trip north.

Lin Ming-na also was weak, but made the trip to the village in comparatively good shape. Two days after arriving, Ming-na had regained most of his strength, under the care of three village women, Kalapoo, her daughter Lakslii and niece Kuneki.

The women lived in one of the smaller houses of the village, a collection of seven houses. The average house was 60 feet square and 20 feet high. Several families shared general living quarters in a house, but each family had its own private space and hearth, separated by a shoulder-high wood partition. The houses were built of board split from logs from nearby cedar trees.

"He is a strange looking man," Kuneki said of Ming-na, dropping several hot stones from the fire into a barrel to keep the water hot.

"Yes, and so is this sickly one," responded Lakslii. She was preparing to give Hin-qua another bowl of a broth made from potato roots and salmon berry sprouts.

"Their clothes are very strange," giggled Kuneki, who wore a dress made from cedar tree bark.

Cave of Secrets

"And their hair, too," said Lakslii, pointing to the men's pigtails.

Young and unmarried, Kuneki and Lakslii would normally not have attended to the ill male strangers, but most of the older, married women were away at one of the other two summer villages for a potlatch. They were both near 17 and first cousins and had been happy to help Kalapoo care for the strangers.

Kuneki's mother and father were from the Sooes village and had left her with her aunt while they traveled to the potlatch. Lakslii's father, Cunnyha, had died the previous season in a whaling accident trying to sew shut the mouth of a harpooned whale to keep it from diving. This was a technique learned by Lakslii's father from his father. On this occasion the whale jerked his head knocking Cunnyha unconscious.

As Kuneki bent to give broth to Ming-na, he turned his head toward his friend and said, " Hin-qua, you must get better; drink some broth. You can't leave me alone in this foreign land." Hin-qua did not respond.

"What a strange language," said Kuneki, "but he's certainly well built and handsome," she giggled. She quickly regained her composure as her aunt returned.

****

A day later Hin-qua was dead. Ming-na wept as the natives prepared for what he thought would be a ground burial typical of his Chinese homeland. Instead, one of the men, Tetacus, as best Ming-na could understand his name, supervised some of the women in wrapping the body in a fetal position. Then to Ming-na's dread, the group carried the wrapped body to a cedar grove some distance away and raised the wrapped body up into a large tree. This was their custom, Ming-na thought, not strong enough to object.

****

Within the week, Ming-na recovered, attracting stares and laughs from the villagers in the makeshift clothes Kalapoo had provided him. Kuneki asked her aunt if she could continue to care for the man and was told that after this day she must be prepared to return to her own village with her parents.

Kuneki had been trying to teach Ming-na some of their language, but it was difficult. In turn, he was trying to communicate with her, and that was even more frustrating. Hand gestures and head nodding with an occasional grunt were the norm. At least each of the five villages had a common language, so Ming-na was not confused between Lakslii and Kuneki's pronunciations.

"How long have I been here?" Ming-na tried to ask Kuneki, who was patiently trying to understand and quite obviously enjoying the interaction.

It was equally obvious to Kalapoo that Kuneki was developing more than just a nurse's interest in Ming-na. Kalapoo thought it was not a good idea to encourage Kuneki's presence much longer. It was good that her parents were returning from the potlatch.

"Look, he points to his chest and gestures to the sun. What is he saying?"

"Perhaps, he is telling us he's a sky god," Lakslii said with a laugh.

Kuneki laughed too. "Yes, maybe he is. The men who found

him said he and his people were from a great canoe that blew out of the sky."

****

After Kuneki returned to her village, Kalapoo and her daughter Lakslii took care of Ming-na. It was obvious to Kalapoo that he missed her niece. He asked about her often. She also realized they must decide at which hearth Ming-na would reside now that he was fully recovered. She intended to discuss the matter with Tetacus when he returned.

As soon as some of the men Ming-na recognized returned from a whaling trip, Ming-na tried to tell them he wished to return to the spot where he had been found.

"What is he trying to say?" said Tetacus, gesturing to the other men and then to Kalapoo who was watching the encounter.

He realized he was not ready to communicate in their language. Then he had an idea. He found a stick and began sketching in the dirt at the feet of Tetacus. He drew pictures of the sea, the rocks and the junks. His rendition of the junks was poor. They looked more like large birds than ships with sails.

"He keeps pointing south and drawing pictures of what looks like water and a very big canoe. Not like our canoes, but much larger and with feathers sticking out," responded a man named Nisga'h.

"What a strange man, indeed. And what a strange canoe!" said another man. Kalapoo just shook her head.

Finally, in desperation to communicate, Ming-na started walking and waving for them to follow. "I think he wants us to come with him and go back to where we found him," said

Tetacus.

"Are you sure?" several of the men said.

Tetacus hunched his shoulders, as much to say it was his best guess. Then he turned to Ming-na.

"All right," Tetacus nodded to Ming-na. "Tomorrow at low tide, Nisga'h and I will go with you." He didn't know if Ming-na understood.

Ming-na nodded in apparent understanding. "Thank you," he said to Tetacus in the language he learned from Kuneki.

Tetacus smiled and said "Ni-how-ma." This is what he thought he knew from Kalapoo to mean "thank you" in the strange man's language.

Ming-na was elated. He had thought about returning for several days now. He knew in his heart that he would not find the other two ships at anchor. By now they would have continued on with or without the treasures. But he had to be sure.

****

The small Chinese man and the two Makah left early the next morning at low tide and completed the trip to the site of the wreckage in about two hours.

As Ming-na had feared, there were no ships to be seen. Most of the evidence of the wrecked Shangti was long gone. He avoided looking at what he thought were probably some scattered skeletal parts. These were now picked clean, beginning to bleach, and no longer recognizable as his crewmates. A few shreds of clothing clung to some of the bones.

He talked to himself. "If they did return, would they have tried to find the three chests? They would not have known

Cave of Secrets

where to look."

"He is crazy," said Tetacus to Nisga'h, "talking to the wind."

"Look, he wants us to follow him toward the cliffs," said Nisga'h. "Should we?"

Ming-na thought he could find the way and with the natives' help, climb up and see if the cave was still partially open and whether anyone had ventured inside. Perhaps the ships had returned and found the cave with its treasure.

They seemed to be following him. With the previous day's good weather drying out the banks, the short climb to the outcropping was easy. Again aloud, as if to himself, "Yes, here it is!"

The two Makah were by now caught up in Ming-na's excitement and sensed that he might not be as crazy as they had thought.

Being careful not to start any slides and gesturing to his two companions to stop short of the large rock, Ming-na lowered himself down to another small ledge where he could see no one had been there since the disaster. The cave opening was, if anything, slightly larger.

"I am going to try and get in there," he said to Tetacus. Tetacus understood.

With that, Ming-na swung down and landed feet first inside the cave entrance. He couldn't see much but the smell of decaying bodies was overwhelming. He crawled back out and after some effort convinced Tetacus and Nisga'h that he needed some light and wanted them to follow him.

The two Makah were not sure they wanted to follow Ming-na into the dark opening, but they did understand about the light. They gathered dry grass on the side of the bank, soaked it in whale oil and, using a flint, were able to fashion a torch. Ming-na could now see much more clearly.

Of the three chests, the two with gold Zhu coins had been badly damaged by rocks from the slide. Coins lay in scattered piles. The other chest, which Ming-na knew contained a large urn, was slightly cracked. Its top hung open. It was his first sight of the urn. It had been sealed in the wooden chest.

The urn appeared undamaged. It was a beautiful blue with painted trees and what looked like footprints. Ming-na, unable to read, did not understand the Kai-shu characters. The wooden chest had similar symbols and characters painted on its sides.

"Come see the treasures," sticking his head out the hole and beckoning to the two Makah.

They were unconvinced, so Ming-na gathered several of the coins and climbed back to the opening to show them. He was thankful to get some fresh air.

The coins gleamed in the sunlight and got their attention. Tetacus fashioned another torch and ventured in, but he stopped short, smelling, then seeing the decaying bodies.

"No, this is a place of the dead and we must leave," he said.

At the same time, Nisga'h was yelling from outside that the tide was coming in and shortly the path they had taken would be under water.

Ming-na ignored the gyrations and continued to gather gold coins, handing them to Tetacus and then when he thought that Tetacus was about to pull him out, he lunged to retrieve the urn. He knew it must be something to treasure. As he did, the round top fell on a rock and broke in several pieces. Nisga'h continued to yell and gesture at both men.

"We must get down fast and we must head back soon," pleaded Tetacus. Finally Ming-na seemed to understand.

Carefully they made their way back down the embankment. Tetacus stepped in some lose gravel and started to lose his

Cave of Secrets

footing.

"Watch out," yelled Ming-na, reaching to grab hold of Tetacus.

He caught him just enough to brake his fall and allow Tetacus to regain his footing. Tetacus was surprised at the strong grip of this man.

"Ni-how-ma," Tetacus said, once again using the word he thought meant thank you.

Ming-na nodded and for the first time in a long while, smiled.

****

And so it was that the three men arrived back at the Ozette village just before dark, tired but eager to tell of their exciting adventure. As it turned out, Ming-na would once again return to the site of the wreckage and the cave.

This time, however, the entrance was sealed. He and several of the Makah tried in vain to clear the rocks and mud. It was not to be. On that return journey, Ming-na knew that he would likely not return again. He also realized that his future now lay with the people of the village.

****

As the days passed, Ming-na was slowly adopted into the tribe and in late fall he moved with the rest to the northern village of Deah. Walking along the beach trail he thought of Kuneki. Her village of Sooes wasn't very far from Deah. He

Hal Burton

had left the gold coins at the Ozette village. They held no value for him or his Makah friends, though several women strung necklaces with them. Still, Ming-na looked forward to showing Kuneki the rest of his treasure.

魏Chapter Five

1981 AD

The Boeing 747 broke through the clouds northeast of Mt. Rainier on its decent into Seattle. Chuck Coolridge had been awake since the seat belt sign illuminated and was getting his paperwork back in order to put in his briefcase. The in-flight movie, "Gallipoli," had just ended. He hadn't watched it. Instead he worked on his notes continuously since the flight left Narita Airport in Japan.

The woman next to him was excited about the film, telling him several times about its young star, Mel Gibson.

He had nodded off for a few minutes, but the stirring next to him woke him up. His briefcase barely closed, and with some difficulty, he got it under the seat. He raised the window shade.

Looking out he could see Lake Washington and the campus of the University of Washington. It was a hazy day, not untypical of an August afternoon in Seattle.

Soon the plane turned for its final approach into Seattle-Tacoma International Airport and Chuck looked out to the west to see the sun setting behind the Olympics Mountains.

In a few days he would be over there somewhere, he thought. The plane landed smoothly and he headed to Customs. He was eager to get started. What he had uncovered in his work during the flight now made his chances of success much greater.

Waiting for him at Customs were three cases stuffed with files from the weeks of study and research in Taipei. His briefcase bulged with notes and he made quite a sight struggling through the Customs checkpoint. Finally his suitcase arrived.

He hoped Karen was meeting him. Sure enough, when he cleared Customs, there she was. Karen Black was the picture of health, dark brown hair and bronze skin. She was a couple of inches shorter than Chuck but definitely his equal in enthusiasm for whatever was their current project. They shared a love of history and the outdoors.

She was eight years his junior. At first, Chuck had been concerned about the age difference, especially when she kidded him about his poor eyesight and thinning hair. His concerns vanished after their third date.

They had met in Anthropology in graduate school at Washington in 1979. And although Chuck had yet to ask, it was assumed they would marry after he completed his Ph.D.

Karen was on summer break from her history teaching job at Samamish High School in Bellevue, an emerging city across Lake Washington, east of Seattle. The six weeks in Taiwan had been by far their longest separation. They embraced and kissed, oblivious to the crowd.

Karen pulled back slightly. "I've really missed you, Chuck Coolridge."

"Me too," Chuck said and squeezed her again.

They both realized they were putting on quite a show.

Cave of Secrets

"The van's parked on Level 4 so we should be able to load up pretty easily," Karen said. Then she noticed his luggage cart.

"Wow, you do have a lot of stuff and your briefcase looks about ready to burst."

He laughed as he realized how funny he must look, and again ignoring the rush of people, gave her another hug.

"Am I glad to see you." They kissed again and headed for the elevators.

He *had* missed Karen and could hardly wait to tell her all he had discovered. He wanted her to help. He was sure once he told her about everything that she would be eager to do so.

There were about four weeks before the fall quarter at the university, so he didn't have a lot of time. Plus, summer was drawing to a close and the weather along the Olympic coast would soon turn foul. Then again, he knew that Professor Bailey would recognize the significance of what he would propose and he would be granted some extra time.

As soon as they exited airport parking, Chuck started talking about his findings in Taiwan.

"Slow down, Chuck," she said, "I know you're excited, but we've got all night."

He reached across and patted her leg. "Sorry. I've been so caught up in this that I tend to forget that you don't know how many frustrating hours I've spent. I'll go back a week or so and bring you up to date slowly," he said. She squeezed his hand.

****

Hal Burton

1981 AD

The municipality of Beijing, with a population approaching 10 million, sprawls over 6,800 square miles. The Great Wall forms its northeastern boarder.

When the monk Hwui Shan sailed from the northern part of China in 499 AD, Beijing, or Peking as it was called then, already was 500 years old. The population of the capital city in 1981 was near six million and it had been Minister Wang Chin-tsi's home since his parents moved from Miyun when he was 5 years old.

A loyal party member from the days of his youth, Wang had risen fast in the bureaucratic ranks to his position today. He had one of the bigger offices in the government building near the corner of Jichang and Jiang Tai roads, within walking distance of Tiananmen Square. Now 55, his bulk was evidence of too many party dinners. No more the thin youth who had followed Mao Tse-Tung since the war in Manchuria in 1945.

Beijing this August in 1981 was unseasonably warm and the fans in the Minister's office were working overtime but not enough for his satisfaction. So he was not in a good mood when he looked up from his desk to greet Lu.

"So, Lu, you have learned what we needed to know from your spy?"

"Coolridge has finished all of the latter records and although there are a few entries still unclear -------."

He was cut short by the Minister. "Get on with it, Lu."

"Yes, minister as I was saying, most everything is clear except the specifics on the urn which I know is most import-

Cave of Secrets

ant." Minister Wang started to protest again. "But first, my report and then some ideas for your consideration."

Wang didn't say anything in response, but his body language said go ahead. Lu detailed how he had learned, through the female spy Kai-hui in Taiwan, that Coolridge's readings of the remaining records revealed the rest of the story of the voyage.

"The three junks left on schedule in 499 AD as we learned from the writings in Changchun. Coolridge learned that by the end of that year they passed near what is today Vancouver Island in Canada. He knows this because the last court record, dated in early 501, contained entries from the monk Hwui Shan's journal. When they passed what Coolridge had interpreted to be the Strait of Juan De Fuca, near Cape Flattery, they ran into a bad storm which pushed them far south before they reached calm waters."

"During the storm the smaller junk, the Shangti, beached near what Coolridge assumed was a point south of Cape Alava, on the State of Washington coast. Most all the crew were assumed lost and the fate of the four chests unknown. Captain Chung, though, was fairly certain the main section of the Shangti beached in one piece and that section had been where the chests were stored."

The narrative went on even though Lu could tell that minister Wang was highly agitated.

"The urn, Lu, you haven't mentioned anything about that yet!" Chin-tse barked.

"No, but let me finish," Lu implored.

"Faster then."

Lu continued his narrative. "At this point, it appears the two remaining junks put in for repairs and a party, including

Hwui Shan's nephew, was dispatched by land northward to look for any survivors and hopefully locate the chests."

"Here, the secret tape recording Kai-hui made is of poor quality and the court narrative sketchy, but as best Coolridge could determine the two vessels were delayed by ensuing storms. By the time they got to the point of rendezvous, there was no sign of the search party, few signs of the wreckage and no sign of the chests."

"No sign!" Minister Wang was angry.

"None, but they did spend at least another day searching the area."

"How were they so sure of the search area and the point of rendezvous?" the Minister asked Lu, somewhat calmer.

"I assume their navigator charted the approximate location of the wreckage, but if that location was in the captain's log or in the monk's journal, Coolridge hadn't found any evidence before he left Taipei."

"What then?" asked Minister Wang.

Wang shifted his weight and wiped beads of sweat from his forehead.

Lu went on.

"Coolridge found entries in the court record from 501 that the Captain and Hwui Shan, feeling they had no other choice, returned to Tangshan harbor and then back to Changchun late in the year 500."

"But here's the most interesting item. Coolridge speculates the gold Zhu coins may still be somewhere near the spot where the Shangti beached. At least he thinks there's a chance they might be and either way the story fits nicely with his proposed graduate thesis." "Do you think he has any idea of the quantity and value of the coins, let alone the historic value of the urn?" The Minister inquired.

"After all, the urn is priceless and, if it is there, it must be returned to China."

"No, I don't think he has any idea as yet, and as I reported, there wasn't any mention of the urn on the tapes our agent made recently of her conversations with the assistant Hao-tung," Lu said. "We do know that before he left he told the assistant, Hao-tung, he was going to organize a field trip to the westside of the Olympic peninsula in Washington State before the fall term starts."

"What's the area called today? Where does he think the Shangti beached?"

"It's somewhere near what is called the Norwegian Memorial, just south of Lake Ozette."

"Here, let me show you." Lu offered a map to the Minister and then cautiously stepped forward to the desk.

"See here, Lake Ozette is on the Olympic Peninsula, west of the city of Port Angeles. It is quite large and only about one mile inland from the ocean. And here, several miles south, I have marked the site of the so-called Norwegian Memorial."

"Do we have any agents in Washington State?" he asked, waving for Lu to step away. Lu retreated several feet from the front of the desk.

"I have anticipated that, Minister, and quite fortunately we do have agents in Seattle and one with some connections at the University," Lu said with pride.

"Excellent! Quickly get a message to your agents."

Actually there was one trusted agent in Seattle and Lu knew that this agent had recruited one other, whom up to now, hadn't justified the dollars they were paying. His chief field agent Woo Xinghai, based in San Francisco, would have to be contacted quickly. As Lu was thinking about this, Minister Chin-tse went on. "We must be close to Coolridge and his plans. Also give me your plan for how we might get the urn and other valuables back to the People's Republic if in fact this Coolridge should discover the hiding place."

"You still assume, Minister, that all was not lost at sea and will be found."

"I don't assume, Lu, but we can't take the chance that it might be."

"It's possible that for some reason the chest were hidden away. Why I can't speculate, but we must consider all possibilities. There is no alternative."

"I'll contact our people and have a plan ready for you tomorrow," Lu said.

He turned and left the Minister's office.

****

The Wallingford district of Seattle is just west of the University District and can be reached by driving north on Interstate 5 from the SeaTac airport. Chuck's apartment was on NE 43rd street near the old Wallingford School.

The drive from the airport in Karen's old Chevy wagon took a while but as they drove he told her more of the discoveries he had written to her about and his plans for a field trip to the coast.

After recapping most of his earlier discoveries, he turned to her excitedly just as they took the 45th Street exit off Interstate 5.

"Here's the newest thing I found. I spent most of the flight going over my notes from the last few pages of the records that Mr. Hao-tung and I never finished translating. I located two more references to an urn which we noticed was mentioned once in the early record of the ship's cargo but discounted it as routine. These two later references seem to imply much more significance and somehow relate to the Buddha Gautama."

Sensing her next question, he continued, "I've looked it up and if it's one of the urns with the ashes of Buddha Gautama, locating it would be a major find. According to what I've read, there were eight urns with his ashes that were to be buried after his death in 483 BC. Maybe one was dug up later or, perhaps, there were really nine urns, not eight. Imagine, an urn almost 2,000 years old with the Buddha's ashes buried somewhere on the Olympic coast."

"I can't see how we could find it after all these years, even if it is there," Karen said.

"Well, here's the best news." He went on to tell her that he found what he believed were the navigator's recording of the longitude and latitude where the one junk beached. As best he could interpret, the location was 124 degrees 41 minutes West longitude, by 48 degrees, 1 minute North latitude.

"That's pretty precise," Karen said.

"Yes, I know. That's what's exciting," Chuck said.

"So where does that put it?" Karen asked as she pulled into the apartment parking lot.

"Just below Cape Alava, south of Ozette, but north of Seal Lion Rock. The closest landmark is the Norwegian Memorial. I won't know for sure till we get over there and take some precise readings. That's why I need to get the trip organized and to do that I need to pick a team for the trip fast. There's not much time before school starts and winter sets in."

"I want to go," Karen said turning to look at him.

She couldn't tell if he was happy or not.

"I can help with the search. Remember that summer before we met? I worked on the dig at the Ozette archaeological site. I did a lot of exploring on the beaches south of Cape Alava."

"I remember, and I hoped you'd want to go," Chuck said, sensing her relief.

"Besides now that I'm back I want to stay close, if you get my drift," he said as they unpacked the wagon.

"Great, but just remember, this is your field trip and you'll want to keep your mind on your quest. So no strange ideas on the sleeping arrangements," Karen said poking him in the ribs.

"You can't blame a guy for thinking about it. Anyway, we'll probably have three of four others along so there won't be much privacy."

"Who do you have in mind?"

"Let's get this stuff up to the room first and then I'll explain," Chuck said.

Chuck noticed how clean and neat the apartment was as soon as they entered.

"Looks like someone's been here since I left."

"Gee, I wonder who," Karen said, curtsying.

"Let's have some music while we work."

She turned the radio on to their favorite radio station, KJR.

After two trips they had everything unloaded in Chuck's living room and Karen was pouring them both a cup of coffee.

"Arthur's Theme" was playing on the radio. Karen lowered the sound and sat down next to Chuck.

"Okay, let's hear what you've got in mind," she said handing him his cup.

"For one thing, we'll need someone from the area, maybe a park ranger or one of the new Makah Indian rangers from Ozette. Then I want to consider one of my students from last year, Bryan Hill, and I'll ask Professor Bailey for a couple more recommendations. About five or six, no more."

"That's about it," he said reaching across the table to caress her.

"Watch it," she teased. Chuck laughed, got up and sat beside her. They both rose and he pulled her close.

It was early evening. Knowing this was going to be one of their last chances for total privacy for awhile, they quietly made their way to Chuck's bedroom.

"I see you haven't forgotten the way," he laughed.

The radio softly played a tune from the new Quincy Jones album.

It was almost a full moon and the glow in the bedroom window cradled them.

They woke early the next morning comfortably wrapped in each other's arms. Regardless of what the future held, they had had a wonderful time last night. For the next several days, they would focus on the expedition and Chuck's quest for the gold coins and the urn.

****

Fall was already in the air on the ocean side of the peninsula, but then the weather at Kalaloch seemed always to be changing. It could be foggy and 50 degrees at the beach and only a few miles inland, clear and 70. It was the height of the travel season this summer of 1981 and all of the RV sites were full, as were most of the sites for tent camping.

Helspath looked out the Ranger Station window daydreaming, but also trying to put some finishing touches on the nature talk he would deliver at the campfire tonight. He noticed the sky clouding up. The weather's always a little dicey on this side of the Olympics, he thought.

Two months after graduating from Washington State University in Pullman, Jerry was drafted into the Army. It was 1970. He went to Basic Training at Fort Sam Houston in San Antonio.

The war ended just about the time he finished Basic. As luck would have it, he got his orders to report to Fort Lewis, near Tacoma, Washington.

When Jerry was discharged in 1972, he applied for a job with the National Parks Service. He was thrilled when he got the letter of acceptance to train to be a Ranger. It was an opportunity to combine his education with his love of the outdoors.

His first assignment was to Crater Lake in Oregon, then to two parks in Utah. He hoped to some day serve closer to home. His wish came true three years ago when he was assigned to the park ranger team serving Olympic National Park. Currently, he was working out of the station near Kalaloch.

Jerry let his interest in stamp collecting wane over the years, but when he visited his mom in Aberdeen, his first weekend off at Kalaloch, he brought back his collection.

His hobby wasn't the only thing that suffered from his vagabond life style. He soon learned that a ranger's life is not conducive to long-term romantic relationships. There had been a few interludes, but nothing lasting.

Jerry was 33 and had developed few friends. Since moving

Cave of Secrets

back to the peninsula he had tried to reestablish his friendship with Bill Jenkins. But even with his sister's help, he'd made little headway.

Bill married Kay after she graduated from Aberdeen High School in 1968 and they lived in Forks, where Bill worked at Allen Mill and Lumber. Jerry had been Bill's best man, but later, the gulf between them widened. Jerry was at college and Dave Peterson's disappearance two years before still hung over them.

Even after days of searching by the sheriff's office, the state patrol and park rangers, the mystery remained. It was assumed Peterson was dead.

Jerry and Bill returned several times to search by themselves, but finally even they gave up searching. Dave's parents had long assumed their son was dead and several years ago had moved to Oregon. Even so, the case remained open in the Clallum County Sheriff's files.

But Bill could not forget. Even after 13 years he took time searching near the Norwegian Memorial and north to the cape. Sometimes he went alone, but a few times he'd gone with Willis Grove, a friend from Neah Bay.

When Jerry returned in 1978 both Bill and Kay tried to talk him into joining the searches, but Jerry said no and the distance between them widened.

****

The University of Washington is north and east of downtown Seattle. Part of the campus hugs the shore of Lake Washington. This Friday morning Chuck hurried along toward the 'Quad' where one of the buildings housed the History Department and the office of his dean, Ed Bailey.

Chuck's office was down the hall from Dean Bailey's. Bailey was expecting Chuck and greeted him warmly. After some polite chatter the discussion turned to Chuck's work in Taiwan and the trip he planned to take to the Olympic peninsula. The dean spent much time studying ancient China and he was fascinated with the prospect of a major discovery, especially by someone he had mentored. They had talked briefly on the phone, so much of their discussion was to fill in the details.

He looked over Chuck's list of people for a search team and agreed to the basic plans before being brought up to date on his latest findings. The make-up of the search team would be critical to their success.

"I agree Karen will be a good choice for the team, but I question your motives." He smiled because he knew of their personal relationship, but also realized how important the results of the search could be and concurred that Karen's experience at Ozette would be helpful.

"I think you're right about getting someone from the area and a Park Ranger," Bailey said.

Chuck nodded and Ed Bailey continued: "I've already got a call into the ranger station at Port Angeles. I've asked them to call you back today. The senior man is Brett Foster, he should be calling you." Bailey continued.

"Bryan Hill is a good selection, too, especially because he knows Kai-shu characters." They had discussed what kind of writings might be found. "He's from Port Angles, isn't he?"

"Yes, and I think he's home for the summer."

"Do you have any suggestions for anyone else? I'd like to have at least five or six people."

Ed Bailey nodded. "Well, now that you mention it, I talked

with Maria Lee today and I think she would be a good addition."

"Who's she, and how did she find out about this?" asked Chuck, a little peeved.

"Now hold on, Chuck, before you get upset," said Bailey. "Don't you remember her, she was in several of my graduate classes in 1978. She teaches at Seattle University."

"No, and I still don't understand," Chuck said, somewhat frustrated.

"She called me this morning and asked about your trip to Taiwan. I mentioned it to her at a conference in Portland last month. I didn't give her a lot of details, but she sounded interested in your field trip. She's been on a couple of digs in Idaho and she does have her masters in Chinese history. She has a couple of weeks before classes start again."

"All right. I guess I do recall her now. Isn't she Korean?"

"I think so, but I met her mom once and it seems to me she was from Russia. But I think I heard her dad was Korean."

"Okay," said Chuck, "give me her phone number and I'll give her a call."

Ed Bailey could still tell that Chuck was reluctant. "Still got a problem with her?" he asked.

Chuck explained his concern about having enough time to get in contact with everyone and still have time for the search before the fall term started.

Bailey quieted his fears by telling him that the magnitude of the project outweighed any time constraints. So getting the best team, even if it took longer, was far more important.

"That would make four in your group, plus a Ranger, but I do have one final suggestion for your team," Dean Bailey said.

"Who's that?" Chuck asked warily.

"You should have a Native American from the region. You likely will have to go on reservation land or at least near some of their ancient sites and it would be good politics, plus they might know the search area."

"Good idea," said Chuck. "I'd had thought about that, too and maybe the park rangers can help there. I'll get on that," he said as he finished his coffee and headed for his own office.

****

Chuck's office was smaller than the Dean's, but just down the hallway and convenient to the department library. He was in the midst of sorting through weeks of accumulated mail when the department secretary, Jane Nolan, poked her head in his office. He had a call from a Mr. Foster of the park rangers. Chuck thanked Jane and reached for the phone.

"Mr. Foster, this is Chuck Coolridge, thanks for getting back to me so soon."

"Sure. I've got some good news," Foster said. "I contacted all my men in the area and Ranger Jerry Helspath volunteered. He's originally from Aberdeen and is working out of the station at Kalaloch. But there's a hitch."

"What's that? He sounds like a real good choice if you'll give him some time off," Chuck said.

"I will because your search could embellish our story of the Olympics. Maybe you'll write a book some day, too, but he has the special condition, not me."

Chuck wondered what he'd gotten himself into. "What's he want?" "Actually it may help. He has a childhood friend who lives in Forks who knows every nook and cranny of the beach where you're going. He's sure he would want to help."

"What's his name?"

"Bill Jenkins. He works at Allen Mill in Forks and, oh yea, he's married to Jerry's sister."

"Okay, if this Jenkins wants to come along, tell Helspath all right, and tell him to call me here tomorrow. I'll be at the office all day. I'll give him all the details of where I think we'll meet, times and everything."

"Now, there's something else that's come up," Chuck stated.

"What's that?" Foster asked.

"It's Professor Bailey's idea and a good one. I'd like to include an Indian from the area, maybe from the Hoh tribe, or better yet, the Makah."

"That's a good idea. I'll have Helspath get back to you on that too," said Foster. "Even if he doesn't go, but I think he will."

"When's this all going to kick off?"

"Probably Monday, at the lodge at Kalaloch, especially now with Helspath in the picture."

Chuck paused. "I guess that's it for now. Thanks again," he said.

Chuck hung up. Things were beginning to fall into place.

****

Saturday morning Chuck Coolridge rose early and drove to his office on the campus of the University. It was a brisk but beautiful morning in Seattle and he was eager to get things going. He figured he would be plenty busy on the phone making arrangements. As expected, several phone calls were exchanged concerning the trip to the Olympic coast. Coolridge was involved in most of the calls, but he would get one call he had not expected.

That same morning Jerry Helspath called his sister's home in Forks. It was just before 8 o'clock. Jerry hoped he would find Bill home. It was not a workday, but he remembered Bill liked to get up early and jog every morning. At least he assumed he still did. Sometimes Bill worked Saturday, although Allen Mill was not running at full capacity lately with the downturns in the industry. All the news analysts were saying now that Ronald Reagan was President, things would improve. Jerry wondered, as many in Washington did. Jerry knew that Bill had strong feelings about the environmental stuff and especially, in Bill's words, "all this Spotted Owl crap."

There had been a few Spotted Owls nailed to trees in the Forks area and it was a touchy subject, one of the sore points between Bill and Jerry.

Jerry could see Bill's point. If your livelihood depends on harvesting trees and a few endangered Spotted Owls prevented you from cutting down trees, you were bound to be biased. As an environmentalist and a naturalist, Jerry saw the other side. He and many of his fellow rangers walked a tightrope when the subject came up. Either way, the Northern Spotted Owl had been designated an endangered species and Jerry was bound to support the law.

After a few rings, the familiar voice of his sister came on the line.

"Hello".

"Hi, it's Jerry."

"Hi stranger, and how are you big brother?"

"Just fine and sorry I haven't talked to you guys lately. I feel bad I missed Bill Junior's birthday party, but I had to go to a conference in Olympia last week."

"That's okay, he missed his uncle, but thanks for the Savings Bond and the postage stamp album," she said sincerely, although she was disappointed Jerry didn't at least come up the next day.

She started to comment on the album, but Jerry spoke first.

"Say, Sis, is Bill there? I need to talk to him."

"He's here. He just got back from his run. Hold on I'll get him. And Jerry, let's get together soon, okay?"

He could hear her call Bill and in a few seconds he was on the line.

"Hi Jerry, long time. What's up?"

"Hi yourself. As I just told Kay, I'm sorry I missed the birthday party. As far as what's up, well I've got a chance to be part of a field trip to the coastal area just south of Ozette. Actually it's sort of a treasure hunt."

"A treasure hunt. You've got to be kidding?" Bill said laughing.

"No, I'm serious," Jerry said. "This guy from the U is organizing it. He's trying to find evidence of a shipwreck hundreds of years ago. Maybe find part of the cargo. I know it sounds weird, but it might be interesting so I'm thinking of volunteering."

"So how the hell did you get involved?" asked Bill, now realizing his friend was serious.

"My boss called all the Ranger stations looking for someone to go with this bunch. A lot of the search will be in the park and get this, the focus of the search area sounds like it's near the Norwegian Memorial." Bill thought to himself, "my god what's this got to do with me."

Jerry sensed Bill's ambivalence.

"Look you can guess why I might volunteer, yes, I know, it might open the whole thing up again, but here's the thing. I told my boss I would go if I could ask you to come along."

"Jeez, Jerry, I finally gave up looking this summer. I've been trying to get on with my life. Now you want me to go on some wild goose chase just in case we might find something about Dave."

Jerry started to say something, but Bill went right on.

"What if this guy finds out about us and what happened in '66 and puts two and two together," Bill argued. "I'd be pissed if I found out we had ulterior motives."

"Who cares? As long we help him, it shouldn't make a difference and we might get lucky. If we go, I may call Sheriff Maxwell too, just to let him know," Jerry said.

Bill was momentarily silent. Then.

"So when's this supposed to happen? I'll have to ask the boss about a few days off and Kay needs to know how long I'd be gone," Bill said.

"As it stands, next week." Jerry replied. "I believe there's a planning meeting scheduled Monday morning," he added.

"Well okay, maybe I should go. But if I do, no talks about endangered species, okay?" he said with a chuckle.

"I promise not to mention owls or trees or anything remotely related," said Jerry. And Bill, call me back as soon as you can if it's a go. Who knows, maybe the trip will do us both some good. I'd sure like to have that good friend back," Jerry said.

"Me too Jerry."

"By the way, young Bill really likes the new stamp album. You'll have to come over and give him some pointers."

****

The phone rang in Chuck Coolridge's office about 10 am Saturday, but it wasn't Jerry Helspath. Setting his cup of coffee down, Chuck reached for the phone.

"Chuck Coolridge," he answered in his best professional voice.

"Hello, Mr. Coolridge, this is Jason Winslow from the Seattle Post Intelligencer."

Puzzled, Chuck answered, "Yes, how can I help you?"

"You don't know me, but I'm a friend of Bryan Hill's. Bryan and I are good buddies from undergraduate years. At the University Club yesterday, he was telling me about your trip to China and this exploring trip you're going on to the Olympics."

"It sounds quite an adventure and I'd like to cover it for the PI. I'm a feature writer and this would make a good story."

"But we may not find anything," Chuck said, mad at Bryan for blabbing. Fortunately, for the moment, only Karen and Dean Bailey knew everything. If the information about the navigation coordinates got out they would have all sorts of weirdoes descending on them. They certainly didn't need to contend with a bunch of treasure hunters.

The Post Intelligencer was Seattle's morning newspaper and Chuck remembered he needed to take the hold off his home delivery when he got back. He liked to read the paper over breakfast and work the New York Times crossword puzzle. He usually read the paper thoroughly and couldn't remember ever seeing Jason Winslow's byline.

Chuck's pause telegraphed his irritation. "I can sense you're not too happy and a little surprised," Jason said, "but, listen, either way the story can't but help your department. You know, get some alumni to support the school more." This guy sounded like a cheerleader, Chuck thought, but maybe he had a point.

"So what do you want, an interview?" Chuck said, trying to sound pleasant.

"No, no, I want to come along!"

"You're kidding," said Chuck. Winslow wasn't.

After another five minutes of conversation, Winslow finally convinced Chuck that he wouldn't be in the way, besides an extra hand might help.

"Tell you what," Chuck said, "let me talk to my dean and I'll call you back."

****

A short conversation with Dean Bailey convinced Chuck that the publicity couldn't hurt. They agreed to let Winslow come along only if he held his story until the search was finished. A few minutes later he dialed the number Jason had given him and was put through to his desk.

"Jason Winslow."

"Okay," said a somewhat frustrated Chuck, you can come along. Let me give you a few details about where we're going to meet and some of the conditions you'll encounter so you'll know what gear to bring along."

"How about my car?" said Winslow.

"There's a parking area where it should be safe," said Chuck. Then he added, "And be sure to be on time."

****

Cave of Secrets

Deah had been one of the five permanent villages of the Makah. Today it is called Neah Bay. The city of Neah Bay is at the end of Highway 112 in the northwest corner of the Olympic Peninsula on the Makah Indian reservation.

Willis Grove had lived in Neah Bay most of his life. So had his parents and their parents and many generations before. Will was now 33 and, like many of the Makah, white skinned and fair-haired.

This Saturday morning when the phone rang Will had just finished taking a group of tourists through the Cultural Center. He was always glad to lead a tour so he could exercise his leg. Will's slight limp was the only clue that he'd had polio as a boy. He was self-conscious about it, and over the years had become a physical fitness nut. He also liked food and constantly fought a weight problem.

His wife complained about all the exercising and the hiking trips, one of the problems they were working out.

"Hello, Will Grove speaking."

"Will, this is Jerry Helspath."

Jerry had known Willis Grove for a couple of years. They first met him when Will spoke at a Clallam County Historical Society meeting in Port Angeles in 1979.

Will worked for the Park Service for a while, but was now working at the Makah Cultural Center in Neah Bay. He had recently been asked to be one of the Makah Indian Rangers, patrolling the Ozette archeological site after the back filling.

About 500 years ago, a catastrophic landslide buried the Makah whaling village at Ozette. Centuries of tidal erosion had finally revealed the site in 1970. For several years, it was the headquarters for an archaeological dig by students from Washington State University.

When Federal funding ran out, several of the Makah were

recruited to guard the area from looters. Excavation had stopped in June and the site would shortly be cleared of any structures and abandoned by the university.

Will Grove had immediately come to mind when Craig Foster asked Jerry.

They had kept in touch since 1979 and he remembered that Will and Bill had known each other, too. He also thought Will and Bill had hiked the area south of Ozette.

Will was quite a character. He was considered an *alien* by some of the Makah because his mother had married a Quileute. The older tribal members will remember the alien origin of the paternal line. In more modern times, they are forced to admit the Makah status of the offspring.

He often spoke at cultural meetings and everyone got a kick out of his talks on totems, especially his own family's unusual Totem. Jerry had always meant to ask him more about it. Among the locals Will was often referred to as, "the totem man."

"Jerry, how are you. What's up, haven't seen you in a while?" Will said.

"I know," said Jerry, "but something's come up. I need a favor. If you've got a minute let me tell you about it. It's a weird story but you might get a kick out of it. I hope you'll want to be involved."

Jerry told him how he'd gotten the call from Craig Foster, the story about Chuck Coolridge's trip and his discovery of the possible shipwreck of a Chinese junk off the coast south of Cape Alava centuries before. Then about Coolridge's quest to find artifacts and his Ph.D. work at the U.

Neither Helspath nor Foster knew about the potential for finding gold and other treasures. At least not yet.

Will responded slowly and somewhat humorously.

"You've got to be kidding. Even if there were such a shipwreck, everything would be long gone now. You know that Bill and I have gone over that section of the coast many, many times, looking for clues to Dave Peterson's disappearance, and, as far as I know, Bill's never found anything like that."

"I know," said Jerry, "but the ocean can change the face of the seashore in one season, so you never know. I have to agree though that looking for stuff over 1,500 years old is stretching it. Anyway, I asked Bill and he I are going to join the search team and Foster says it would be good politics to have a Native American along and – ah"

"Okay, I get it," laughed Will, "I'm the resident Indian for this gig. Hum. You never know I might get some tidbits for my talks and maybe even something for the Center. Hey, but what about you and Bill. Does this Coolridge know about what happened in '66?"

"No, at least I don't think so, but I'll probably tell him. I'm also going to call Sheriff Maxwell in Forks and let him know about it so there's no problem there."

There was a long pause before Will spoke again. "When is this excursion supposed to happen and what are we talking about in terms of time?"

"I think Coolridge wants to get started this Monday, although I haven't talked to him directly. I think Foster said it might take the week."

"All right," said Will, "I'm in. I can get away for at least three days because I have some time off before I start working part-time down at Ozette. So get back to me with all the gory details. One thing though, I want to be back here in Neah Bay for the Makah Day's celebration, next weekend."

After he hung up, he realized he should have checked with

his wife Janice before committing. They were separated, but he owed her that much. Their consoler had told Will that he needed to stay home more. He'd call her.

****

Later that day Will went next door to his mom's house to tell her he would be gone for three or four days. His dad died the previous year and Will checked on his mom whenever he could. Living next door was convenient.

Will had been separated from his wife for three months now. They were seeing the counselor and things were better. He again reminded himself to call Janice. She was living with her mom in Sekiu.

Will took the short walk up the path to his boyhood home. He was proud of his Makah heritage and, when his mom kidded him sometimes about being a little over weight, he reminded her that Makah means "generous with food."

The name was given to the Makah by other tribes. The Makah were known for their generosity, but Will always twisted the definition a little to fit his situation.

His mom had a good sense of humor and she too was proud of their heritage. She hung many articles from the family's history around the house. She said it was good for them to be reminded of their past. Will was fond of the many woven blankets and the variety of brightly-painted pottery. It was the totem, though, that most fascinated him. His grandfather on his mother's side first told him the about totems, years ago. His grandfather Mike had been one of the most skillful carvers of his day. Cedar trees had been very plentiful and each house not only had a totem pole in front of the house, but as corner posts and many spots inside the house.

His grandfather explained to him that the figures he carved were family crests or often symbolic of some event in mythology. He told Will that their ancestors sometimes took the form of animals, like whales or birds.

Will caught himself daydreaming. Time to get back to the Center. He did remember that his mom had just reminded him the other day that she needed his help to sort out some more things in the attic. She and Clarence had been about finished when he had his stroke.

****

Chuck Coolridge watched out his window as the sun began to drop below Meany Hall just across from his University office. He was beginning to think the call he was waiting for would never come. Time was running out. He had booked two cabin units at Kalaloch for Monday. If he was going to get everyone there in time for a briefing, plus get started early Tuesday with the search, he had to push. He already told Karen to start packing and had a call into Bryan, who he had discovered, was staying with friends in West Seattle.

Frankly, he didn't care whether the reporter Winslow got there in time or not, and he was waiting to telephone Maria Lee as soon as the ranger called to confirm. He also reminded himself to chastise Bryan.

Just when he had just about given up, the phone rang.

"Chuck Coolridge," he answered enthusiastically.

"Professor Coolridge, this is Jerry Helspath from the Ranger Station at Kalaloch."

"Hey, thanks for calling, I was getting concerned. By the way, it's Chuck, okay? I have a feeling we'll get to know each other pretty well if you're calling to tell me what I hope you are."

"Yes," said Jerry, "you've got that right."

Jerry explained to him that he was on board and that he had gotten one of the new Makah Rangers, Willis Grove, to join the group. Also that he had heard back from his friend Bill Jenkins. "He'll join us too if that's still okay."

"That's great," said a relieved Chuck Coolridge. Helspath then asked about the schedule.

"So I understand you want to get started Monday morning?"

"Yes," said Coolridge, "As early as possible."

"So fill me in and I'll call Will Grove and Bill for you. Monday will be here before you know it," Jerry said. "Will Grove can bring his truck and maybe pick up Bill Jenkins in Forks if that works out."

"Great, said Chuck, we will meet on Monday morning at Kalaloch."

"At Kalaloch. That's perfect for me, but then I guess you knew that," said Jerry.

****

John Yang had a sense of great accomplishment. Finally after all these years of paying for insignificant information, they would finally get their moneys worth. It was a fact of life today. Spying for altruistic reasons was past for most. No longer were there many righteous believers, no signing on for political principles. Money, that was the main motivator.

A few like John still clung to their beliefs and genuinely hated the enemy.

Now he had his spy on Coolridge's team. He knew that the money was all that mattered, but Beijing didn't care. They wanted results. And how about his friends in the FBI? He hadn't heard from them. Probably weren't the least interested in Coolridge's expedition. Actually, he reminded himself, there's no reason for them to even know about it. Their money he didn't mind taking.

The FBI paid him well for any information he gave them about Taiwan. As the Taiwanese consulate in Seattle, John Yang was involved in both exports and imports. Sensitive information often passed through his office. Of course, his true loyalties were with Beijing. When the message came about Coolridge, he had contacted his spy immediately. The rest had been surprisingly easy. His superior, Woo Xinghai, would fly into Portland from Los Angeles. John would have to get a room in the Ocean Shores area. But that shouldn't be a problem.

Chapter Six

It was Monday morning in Beijing and Minister Wang Chin-tsi was impatient. His morning meal had not settled and he was wishing he hadn't had that extra helping of rice. He definitely was beginning to show signs of overindulgence and felt the pressure from the up and coming younger party members.

He knew he had to have something to show his superiors that he was still very much in control. The opportunity of finding the ancient urn and the gold would be perfect.

Chin-tsi had expected Lu Xun at any moment. He reflected on the events of the past day.

The "control" for the few agents they had in the western United States, Woo Xinghai reported yesterday. He made contact with John Yang in Seattle again and would report back today, which was still Sunday in Washington. Furthermore, the control himself would be flying into Portland from Los Angeles and meeting the ship.

This was part of the plan that senior foreign agent Woo and Lu Xun were putting into action. Close contact once Coolridge's trip started was imperative. They were finalizing the plan for returning the gold treasure and the urn to the People's Republic, if it was found. Just then his secretary announced agent Lu.

"Yes Lu, what do you have for me?"

****

The Denney's restaurant on 45th street in the Wallingford District was crowded with the after-church crowd so Coolridge and Dean Bailey had to wait for a table.

"Thanks again for meeting me today, Doctor Bailey," said Chuck when they were finally seated. "I've got my crew together and wanted to go over some of the details with you." He passed the list of his expedition members, with a footnote about Jason Winslow.

                 Team Members - Ozette Trip:

           Chuck Coolridge ----- Team Leader
           Karen Black ------- History Teacher
           Bryan Hill -------- Graduate Student
           Jerry Helspath ---------- Park Ranger
           Bill Jenkins ------ Helspath's friend
           Willis Grove ------- Makah Ranger
           Maria Lee -------- Seattle U Teacher
           Jason Winslow -Reporter, Seattle PI

"That's quite a list. You sure that's not too many?"

"It's about two more than I'd planned, but then there's Maria Lee and this Jason guy from the P-I. I'm still upset with Bryan, but maybe we could use the publicity. Anyway he knows about it and I told him where we're going to meet to get started so if he shows up, so be it."

Bailey asked a few more questions and then, "You know, the more I think about this the more I am concerned about what happens if you find something."

Chuck nodded.

"Okay, I guess we're committed," Bailey said.

"And you're off for Kalaloch then."

"Yeah, we leave this afternoon."

****

As Lu Xun finished his report in Wang Chin-tsi's office, the normally stoic Minster's face broadened in a smile. It couldn't have been better news.

"So an agent from Seattle is on the expedition team. Excellent! But your plans for retrieval, if it is to be made, are still not firm. Let me help you with that by calling Minster Wu Chong and your superiors."

As far as Lu was concerned, the plans were firm. He knew from experience that he had to let the Minister feel he was in control.

"Have someone from your staff check on other ships along the Pacific Coast that we've used before. Several will do our bidding for the right price."

"Captain Varney has been reliable before," Lu said.

The Minister was uncharacteristically quiet. It was true, Varney had been reliable before and he happened to be on the West Coast of the United States.

"Still, we may need a backup ship at our disposal if your plan is to succeed. You have no time to spare, Lu, so let me check on a backup ship for you. In the meantime, proceed with Varney."

"Yes, Minister." said a relieved Lu.

"Remember," the Minister added, "everything must be in place by this time tomorrow, which is Monday morning in the western United States."

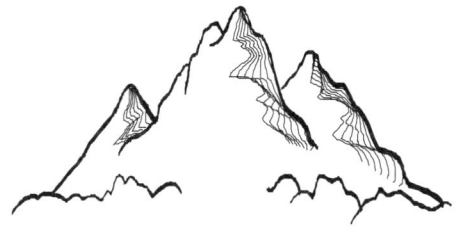

Chapter Seven

There are only a few places to stay along U.S. Highway 101 heading north toward Lake Ozette, unless you go all the way to the city of Forks. Chuck wanted somewhere to meet close to Rialto Beach and Lake Ozette, but central enough for everyone to reach by early Monday morning, and with space for a large group.

Lake Quinault Lodge was one possibility. Then there was a cabin near Queets, but Chuck had settled on Kalaloch. Now that Helspath had joined the crew, his choice had seemed even more appropriate. Kalaloch is about halfway between the coastal villages of Moclips and LaPush. It consists of a campground and recreational area with a store and gas station. On the ocean side is Kalaloch Lodge and several cabins spaced along the beachfront. North and south from the lodge, several beaches offer fishing, clamming and occasional glimpses of migrating whales.

Chuck, Karen, Bryan and Maria Lee stayed Sunday night in the two cabins reserved by Chuck, dividing up with Chuck and Bryan in the larger one. Their room would serve as the meeting room in the morning. The four of them ate in the Lodge's restaurant, which was known for it's excellent menu.

Cave of Secrets

Their table offered a fabulous view of the ocean beach. The beach, especially in front of the Lodge, was densely covered with a maze of sun-bleached and surf-polished logs. Chuck thought about the days ahead and whether their quest would be successful. He looked at his three companions.

"What a great evening," Chuck said to them, but with a smile and wink for Karen.

Karen smiled back. "Yes it is and too bad we have to all get up so early tomorrow."

Any plans Chuck may have had for another night alone with Karen vanished when she rose from the table, gave him a wink in return and, with Maria in tow, wished Bryan and Chuck good night. Maria had been a pleasant surprise and she got along well with Karen.

When the two men got back to their cabin they were alone for the first time that day.

"Bryan, I'm a little upset about you telling Jason Winslow about this trip."

"I'm sorry Chuck, we were at this party at the Club, and I got started talking about----."

Chuck held up his hand.

"Let's forget it," Chuck said.

"In the long run, if he shows up, the publicity will help the University. Just next time check with me first."

He reached into the cooler by the dresser.

"So, let's have a beer and you can help me put these information packets together," Chuck said.

It was then that he noticed the blinking red button on the house phone. Chuck lifted the receiver and pressed the button. "Yes, Front Desk."

"My light was flashing. This is Chuck Coolridge in Cabin 3."

"Yes, Mr. Coolridge, you have a message to call Professor Bailey at home as soon as possible."

The phone in the cabin was only for room-to-room calling, so Chuck told Bryan he was going to the Lodge to call Professor Bailey.

****

"I take it you and Chuck have gone together for a while," Maria asked, as Karen emerged from the bathroom.
"Yes, for some time."
"Do you have someone special in your life?" Karen said.
"No." Maria didn't add any details.
"How about family close by?" Karen continued.
"My mother and father live in Tacoma." Maria hesitated, as if to add something, then turned toward the bathroom.
"Guess it's my turn," she said.

When the door closed, Karen crawled into bed. At dinner their conversation had been animated. Now it seemed forced. Maybe it was just her, but Maria seemed more guarded. It was probably just the hour and the awkwardness of the close quarters.

****

After an early breakfast at the Lodge, Chuck's cabin was readied for the meeting, scheduled to start at eight or as soon as everybody got there. Kalaloch was about an hour drive south from Forks, but two hours from Will Grove's house. Will was picking up Bill Jenkins on the way.

Jerry Helspath was the last to arrive, having had to attend to a couple of things at the nearby Ranger Station before he could get away.

It was nearing eight when Chuck decided it was time to get started. The reporter wasn't there yet. "Too bad," Chuck thought.

He was on edge this morning, still mulling over Bailey's call. He hadn't had a chance to tell Karen about it. Maybe he wouldn't. Bryan hadn't asked and had been fast asleep when Chuck returned. He recalled Bailey's words, "it turns out that your assistant, Hao-tung, has a lady friend that's an agent for the communists and the FBI ----

"Chuck are you going to get started?" Karen's question brought him back to the present and he made his way to the front of the room.

"There's more coffee and I've got some donuts for later, so let's get started."

Thanks for coming. By now you've all met. You'll get to know each other better, after three or four days of hiking and camping," he chuckled.

"Before I talk about the background for this trip and its potential, I want to give you our schedule so if you want to give your relatives or people at work a little better idea of when you'll be back, you can."

Chuck asked Karen to pass out an informational packet and started talking again. "We should leave here in about two hours. I've brought two University vans. Those, plus Will's truck, should be enough for all of us and our gear."

"We'll be setting up at Mora campground which, for those that don't know, is about a mile inland from our departure point at Rialto Beach. There's a Ranger station with a phone at Mora, too. Once we get there and finish set up we won't have a lot of time before dark. Bill Jenkins was kind enough to drive over to Rialto and Mora for me yesterday and reserve a good camp sight. Still, we need to get set up before dark."

"Yes, Jerry," seeing Helspath's raised hand.

"Do you really think we'll be there for three or four days?"

"Maybe more, but my best guess is that we won't be there over three days because it's not all that big an area to cover with three search teams. Besides, after three days if we haven't found anything, it's probably not to be found." Chuck, of course, was pretty sure he could narrow down the search area once he got close.

"So if there's no more questions for now, get another cup of coffee and I'll tell you a story about a Chinese Junk that went aground on our Washington coast about 1,500 years ago."

Just then, the door opened. "Hi, I'm Jason, sorry I'm late." The reporter was about 30 with thick brown hair, just touching his shoulders. The face atop his six-foot frame had a permanent, almost boyish grin. He nodded toward Bryan, "Hi, Bryan."

Chuck turned to the team and said, "Some of you knew about the possibility of a reporter joining us for the trip. This is Jason Winslow with the P-I."

Winslow nodded.

"All right, have a seat. You're just in time for the briefing."

Karen rose and handed an info packet to Winslow who, Chuck noticed, gave her a big smile when she sat down. Winslow continued to ogle Karen. Oh, great, and a flirt too he thought. But it was time to get on with his story.

****

When Chuck finished, the faces of his audience ranged from mild puzzlement to disbelief to astonishment. Only one person in the room besides Karen had known the story completely and that person, unknown to Chuck, was on the payroll of the People's Republic of China.

But then Chuck didn't tell the complete story. That would come later when they reached their first nights destination. The information from the FBI about the possible involvement of the communists had him concerned. But then, maybe his so-called exact coordinates weren't so exact. He would check out that first thing tomorrow. Professor Bailey had told him to take the time he needed considering the importance of what he might discover. Yet, he was eager to get going.

Chuck went over to Jason and offered his hand. At this point he figured he might as well be hospitable. "Hi, glad you could make it. Any questions?"

"Thanks." Yea, if I'm going to ride in one of the vans, how about my car?"

Chuck thought for a minute. He thought he had already answered that question.

"You can leave it at the Ranger Station. Jerry can show you and let them know."

He got Jerry's attention and waved him over.

"Anything else," Chuck asked.

"How about my gear?"

"You'll ride with Karen and me, so put your stuff in the blue van."

****

The city of Ocean Shores is on a sandy peninsula that separates Gray's Harbor from the Pacific Ocean. It is a very popular resort and many of the motels require a two-night minimum stay when a weekend is included in the reservation.

The Gray Gull Motel is one of the more popular with tourists and a weekend getaway destination for people from the Seattle-Tacoma area. This was especially true with Labor Day approaching.

John Yang had some difficulty getting a room on short notice. The Polynesian and The Canterbury Inn, also on Ocean Shores Blvd., were booked. The Gray Gull, however, did have a last minute cancellation. John had been lucky.

John's parents were born in Kaohsiung on the island of Formosa, now called Taiwan. Their ancestors had lived on the island for generations, dating back to the time of Japanese occupation in the late 19th century. When the Nationalists arrived in 1949, John, whose Chinese name was Yang Feng, was 9 years old.

The Yangs had strong feelings about what they called the occupation and had been openly pro-Communist, so they struggled under the Nationalist regime. They eventually lost their fishing business to a Nationalist sympathizer. When John turned 19, his parents sent him to live with an uncle in Seattle where he attended Seattle University, graduating with honors. After graduation, he returned to Taiwan to find his parents destitute and his mother ill.

He tried to help them, taking a job with the local tourist bureau, but as his mother's condition worsened his father seemed to give up and Yang's anger increased.

He met several anti-Nationalist people at a local hangout for younger people. Eventually, he came to the attention of a recruiter for the People's Republic intelligence operation.

Before long he became an active participant in their spy network in Taiwan and was groomed by his Communist

Cave of Secrets

superiors to return to the United States where he would be more valuable. He got a job as a clerk in the foreign office in 1963. Within two years he was supervisor over the export-import department in Taichung. John returned to Seattle in 1965 after his parents both passed away. It had been a bitter time.

The Nationalist government had encouraged his return to the U.S. and assigned him to the consulate's office in Seattle. His Beijing contacts couldn't have been happier. What a stroke of luck.

It was a year later when he became the assistant consul. That same year a U.S. government agent contacted him. His name was Steve Collins. Would he let him know when certain Taiwanese companies were shipping machine tools into Seattle? They would pay him for the information. Many U.S. patent protected machine tools were being copied in Taiwan, brought into the U.S. and sold at very low prices. After he consulted with Beijing, he accepted. In 1979 he became the Consul. In his 15 years working at the Consulate he had been able to supply Beijing information on Boeing, Fort Lewis in Tacoma and the Naval Base near Bremerton. At the same time he continued to supply information on imports to agent Collins and this allowed him to enjoy a nice lifestyle. He also had recruited the agent they were to rely on so heavily now, if the plan was to succeed.

****

"Can you hear me Xinghai?" John Yang asked.

Woo Xinghai boarded the S S Monrovia in Portland. He was the senior agent for the western United States. The plan had been hastily put together, but Woo had been able to get a flight into Portland from Los Angeles in time to meet the ship.

The Monrovia was of Liberian registry. Its location on the West Coast, its itinerary and a willing captain were the final links in the plan put together in Beijing.

"Yes, there's some noise, but I can hear," said Woo loudly, trying to overcome the static.

John was using one of the new wireless phones developed by AT&T. They were communicating on a prearranged frequency, but it was not a good connection. He suspected the problem was with the ship's receiver.

"Fine, tell the captain to keep on his present course for the port of Gray's Harbor and I'll contact you again in three hours."

To have a friendly ship in the Pacific, heading for the mill at Cosmopolis in Grays Harbor to take on wood chips was a stroke of luck, Yang thought. The Monrovia's captain was Miles Varney. Varney was a true mercenary. The People's Republic had used him before. His price was high, but he always got the job done. Varney often contracted for legitimate work, too, which turned out to be his reason for being at the right place at the right time.

John put the wireless phone set back in an extra suitcase and then stowed it in the closet. It was still a nice day and he decided to take a stroll on the beach.

He headed toward the nearby public access road, rather than directly to the beach from the back of the Motel. He had seen several signs earlier asking people not to walk through the grassy sand duns behind the motel. The first thing John noticed as he neared the beach were colorful kites that seemed to be everywhere catching the wind from the sea.

Distracted by some men trying to get a huge cone shaped kite airborne, he almost collided with a group of horseback riders sauntering along the water's edge.

As John continued he thought about his own luck several years ago in recruiting such a well-placed agent in Seattle. Communication during the exploration trip would be tricky. In all likelihood there would be no phones near the search area, but, hopefully, the prearranged schedule could be kept for calls to his room at the Gray Gull.

This was the first real test for the Seattle agent and John hoped his efforts in recruiting would pay off on this mission. This was also one of the agents' first major assignments and John wanted to impress Lu Xun and the people in Beijing that the money he had been paying was justified.

Hal Burton

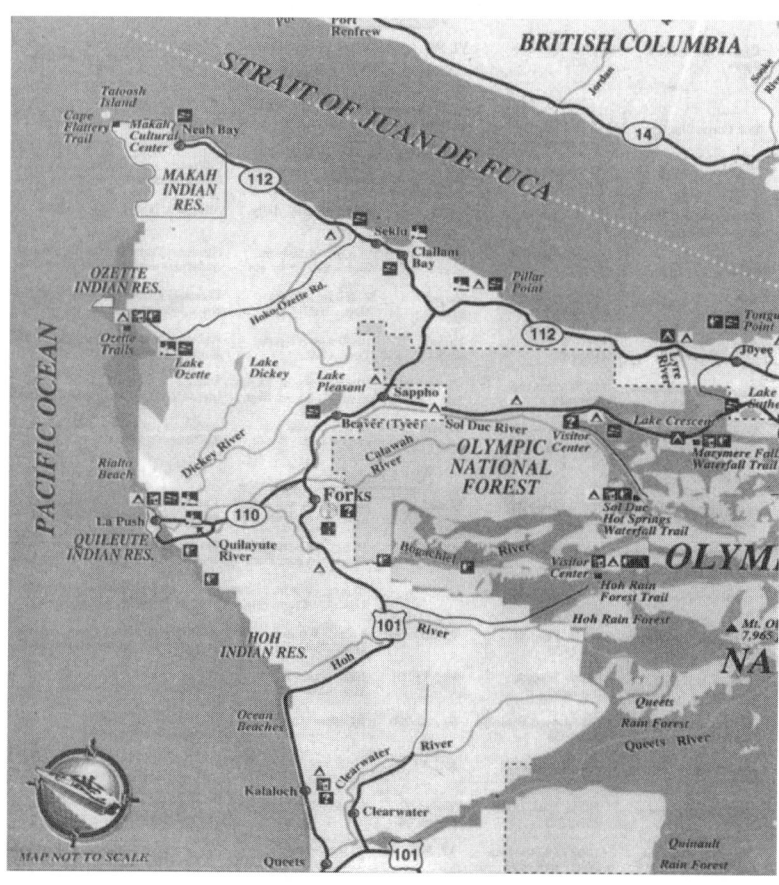

Northwestern Olympic Peninsula circa 1980

Chapter Eight

US Highway 101 hugs the coast line as it leaves Kalaloch, then turns sharply east at Ruby Beach. There it almost parallels the path of the Hoh River, until it turns north again toward the city of Forks. The fog that the caravan ran into cleared as they turned inland. The sun peaked through the fir, hemlock and cedar trees as they crossed the Bogachiel River and turned north to Forks.

Will Grove and Bill Jenkins were in the lead in the truck followed by Chuck Coolridge, Karen Black and Jason Winslow in one of the university vans with Bryan Hill driving the second van with Maria Lee and Jerry Helspath. After stopping for more supplies in Forks, they left Highway 101 and headed west on the road toward LaPush and Rialto Beach.

LaPush is on the Quileute Indian reservation, tucked into a cove framed by tall trees and picturesque beaches. Usually boats from the fishing fleet can be seen entering and leaving the safe harbor. Just to the north is Rialto Beach.

"Remember, Chuck," Karen said, "you don't take the road into LaPush, you stay to the right up ahead to get to Rialto."

The conversations in Bryan's van had been lively. It was more subdued in Chuck's. Karen was trying to find something other than western music on the radio and settled on a Christopher Cross tune.

"Oh, that's appropriate," said Chuck.

"What's that?"

"The song, you know, *Sailing,*" Chuck said.

"Oh, I see, yes I suppose so," Karen said.

Jason, who had been verbose earlier, to Chuck's chagrin, spoke up again.

"I appreciate coming along. I'm fascinated about maybe finding the treasure and solving a mystery. It will make great copy even if we don't find anything and I've got my editor convinced it's a feature story if we find something."

"I do hope we find something," Karen said, "but the urn would be --." Chuck glared at her. Details about the urn had been omitted from his briefing. He had also withheld knowledge of the coordinates he interpreted from the old writings. He had decided to cover those subjects later when he felt more comfortable with the group. He hadn't wanted to get into a discussion on the urn just yet. The gold coins should be enough enticement.

"What urn?" asked Jason. Chuck had no choice now.

He told him about his speculations concerning the ancient urn and its possible connections to a Buddha from the 5th century BC, but quickly added that he doubted whether it would still be in one piece even if they found it. At least the gold coins would be salvageable, he said.

"Wow, this will really make a story!" Jason exclaimed

Chuck ignored the outburst and continued.

"Another thing, in case you're wondering, the authorities in Seattle have been told about the possibility of gold and Dean

Bailey is coordinating with them as to the legalities, salvage laws and so forth."

"In addition, as I mentioned this morning, I'm supposed to call the local Sheriff if we do find anything so we can get security."

"Where's the sheriff from," asked Karen.

"His office is in Forks. I think his name is Maxwell," said Chuck.

"Not many know about our trip over here, but I suspect it won't take long, and I am going to hold you to your promise Jason to keep all this quiet until everything is finished, gold or no gold and urn or no urn – okay?"

Jason paused.

"Sure, I agree, but, say, is that the same sheriff Maxwell who was in charge of the search and investigation when that high school kid disappeared around Ozette back in 1966?"

****

Maria Lee had been quiet except for occasional small talk and was content to listen to Bryan and Jerry discuss everything from the lost treasure to how the Super Sonics would do this year. Lee was about five foot four with jet-black hair, almond eyes, and honey colored skin. She wore what looked to be parts of an army uniform. Jerry and Bryan each silently speculated she had a great figure under her baggy fatigues.

As they left Forks, Maria leaned forward from the back seat and asked Bryan questions about Chuck's trip and their chances of finding evidence of the old shipwreck or the gold coins.

Bryan responded, "Well, Chuck pretty well covered it this

morning. Frankly, I don't think we have much of a chance." Trying to impress her, he continued.

"Of course, with Chuck's information on the coordinates, we should be able to pin down the supposed location within a half mile or so."

"What coordinates?" Maria and Jerry asked, almost at the same time.

"Oh, well, I guess Chuck was going to tell everyone tonight anyway. He thinks he has a fairly precise fix on the shipwreck from the ship's records he got just before he left Taiwan. He made some notes and worked on them during his flight home."

"That should make our search a lot easier," said Jerry.

"Why didn't he tell us about that?"

"Maybe he's not so sure of the exact location," said Bryan.

Maria nodded and then turned her attention to Jerry. At first her questions were just mundane as she asked about his job, how long he had been at Kalaloch and where he went to school. She was somewhat surprised to learn that he had gone to Washington State and majored in Forestry. He also commented on his interest in stamp collecting. She was surprised to learn he was still single. Then her questions got a little more pointed.

"Why did you volunteer for this trip?" she asked.

"All of the rangers in this region were asked by our boss, Craig Foster, to volunteer. Because I'm stationed here and I used to hike the beaches a lot as a kid, I figured, why not."

He looked at her then, as if to say, "how about you?"

Maria sensed from his look that it was her turn.

"Well, as was mentioned last night, my master's degree is in Chinese history. When I talked to Chuck's dean, Ed Bailey, and he told me about this trip, I just couldn't pass it up."

"I can understand that," Bryan chimed in. "But what about you, personally. I don't mean to pry, but you do look Asian. Is that part of your interest?"

Then quickly adding. "Don't get me wrong, you're very pretty and -------,"

Maria interrupted him, "No offense taken," she smiled. "And thanks for the compliment. Yes, I am part Korean, but somehow I ended up studying the Chinese culture. Maybe it's because Korea has been greatly influenced by Chinese history and culture."

She shrugged. "Anyway, that's it," she said.

Jerry smiled and thought here's a real interesting lady, but probably someone with lots of boyfriends. Oh well, might as well find out, he mused.

"Did you guys have to let a lot of people know you'll be gone for several days?" he asked.

"No, just my roommate in Seattle," Bryan said. "My folks are in Port Angeles. I'll call them when we get to Rialto."

"How about you Maria?" Jerry asked.

She smiled and leaned forward. "I called my Mom and let our department secretary know, but that's it," she replied.

Jerry tried not to show his delight.

They continued with small talk and Jerry asked Maria more about her background and job at Seattle University. He had to admit she was fascinating and he was about to get a little more personal when Bryan said, "Here's the cutoff to Rialto, it won't be long now."

****

Back in the second van, Chuck turned to look at Karen. She saw his puzzled look and they both shrugged their shoulders to Winslow's comment about Sheriff Maxwell.

Jason went on with a note of apology. "Sorry, I assumed you knew about it and that's why Helspath and Jenkins are along. It makes sense, since they probably have searched the area dozens of time, especially back in '66 when their buddy Dave Peterson disappeared."

Chuck was listening intently now and beginning to realize that Jerry Helspath had left out a few details of why he wanted to join their excursion.

"According to the old articles at the paper, the case is still open," Jason added. "I did quite a bit of research on the area before I left Seattle."

"Actually," said Chuck trying to conceal his surprise, " I don't know that much about it, suppose you tell us what you know."

****

The conversation had also been lively in Will's old Chevy truck, the lead of the caravan. Bill Jenkins and Will Grove enjoyed being together. It had been some time since they'd seen each other. Will had to keep an eye on the following vans so the group would stay together. They were making good time, but the junction in the road was ahead and he wanted to make sure they stayed right for Rialto Beach rather than left toward LaPush.

"So you and Jerry haven't told Coolridge about the Peterson disappearance?" Will asked.

"No," said Bill. "It was Jerry's idea to wait till tonight after we got to the campsite at Rialto."

Cave of Secrets

"We thought he would balk at taking us along if he knew." Will thought that, if anything, Coolridge would be happy about their knowledge of the area. Jerry and Bill were making too big a thing about it. He turned to Bill.

"But won't Coolridge be upset if you wait too long to tell him. He will find out from the Sheriff soon enough."

"I suppose, but, it was Jerry's idea and I agreed," Bill said.

****

The Ranger Station and Campgrounds at Mora were only a half-mile inland from the beach at Rialto. In a few minutes, they had gathered most of their gear from the vans and went about setting up their campsite.

Jerry and Bill sensed Chuck's coolness and preoccupation as they worked together to set up their tent next to his. For the time being, they put it down to imagination. Still, Bill thought there was more to it. He turned to Jerry and whispered, "What's his problem?"

As Chuck had suggested earlier, the two women were to share one tent; Chuck and Willis, Bryan and Jason, and Bill and Jerry paired in the others. In addition, there was one large tent for eating and meetings and a smaller one for equipment storage. Chores were shared and on this first night, Chuck and Karen prepared the evening meal while the others finished unpacking and exploring. Chuck said they would eat at six and meet afterwards. While Karen was getting a few things organized, he went over to Bill and Jerry's tent.

"Say, Jerry," Chuck asked, " There is something we need to

discuss before you guys wander off before dinner."

"Sure," Jerry answered sheepishly. He assumed they were now going to find out what the problem was.

"Let's take a walk together. This isn't something I want the others to hear right now," he said and moved off toward the path leading to the ranger station.

"You two have not been honest with me or else it's a remarkable coincidence that the two of you were involved in this disappearance back in 1966. The one Jason just told me about in the van. What gives?"

Bill and Jerry fell silent for a moment, then Jerry began to tell the story of Dave Peterson's disappearance.

"Believe me, we were going to tell you. There just never seemed to be a good time, and we thought that if you knew ahead of time you wouldn't let us come along," said Bill. "We already told Sheriff Maxwell and said we would tell you as soon as we got here. Sorry you had to hear it from someone else."

Chuck thought for a moment. "Okay, I guess no harm done and with your background it's probably an advantage. But let's get something straight. Our purpose here is to find evidence of the shipwreck and hopefully find some of the ancient coins. If you do find some clues to Peterson's disappearance, that's a bonus. There's a couple of things I haven't been forthcoming about either. At our campfire meeting tonight, we all need to start with a clean slate. Jerry, I'll expect you and Bill to tell everyone the story, okay?"

Bill and Jerry said thanks and nodded in agreement.

As they walked back to their tent and Chuck went over to Karen, Bill turned to Jerry and quietly asked, "So what hasn't he told us about?"

"I guess we'll find out tonight," Jerry answered.

"Let's finish up and help Karen get the fire started."

****

At 7 o'clock it was still light. There would likely be a beautiful sunset. The western horizon had several layers of cirrus clouds that were already turning a light crimson from the sun's rays.

Chuck and Karen outdid themselves. They cooked the salmon Indian style. The fish was filleted, spread open and attached to metal racks. Then the racks were stuck in the ground around the edge of the fire. A few minutes on one side, then the other and the salmon was ready. Karen had a large fruit salad already prepared and French bread. Chuck offered a chilled Chardonnay.

Everyone took a small serving and then Chuck rose.

"Here's to a successful search. Thanks for being part of the team."

They finished eating and as soon as everything was cleared away, Chuck started the meeting.

"First, here are your team assignments for tomorrow's search. Each day, we'll have someone stay here at our camp to watch over everything and act as a message center."

"The nearest phones are at the ranger station. Tomorrow, Bryan will staff the camp and Karen and Jason will come with me. Jerry and Maria will be the second team and Will and Bill the third. This puts at least one person very familiar with the area on each team along with someone who has been on a dig before."

Chuck continued.

"Each team will have a metal detector and I suggest you use it as much as possible. Any questions on its use, see me before you leave. We will start our search just north of Cape Johnson. The low tide in the morning should give us time to do a thorough search, working our way north."

Karen was moving through the group.

"Karen is passing out some ideas on how to conduct your search. You also have the handout from our meeting yesterday. I would like to leave here no later that 7a.m., because we have a ways to go to get to our starting point. My team will go a little farther north to start. I have some readings to take that should help us be more precise in our search zone. If I can narrow it down some, Karen will hike back and let you know. But for tomorrow morning, I'd like to continue as I've outlined."

While everyone was intent on his next words Chuck said, " before I explain about the sextant readings and another aspect of our search, Bill and Jerry have something to tell you."

****

About 10 minutes later, the story of the mystery surrounding Dave Peterson had been told. Chuck then related his hopes of pinpointing a location using his sextant and the coordinates interpreted from the ancient Chinese logs. He told them about the urn, his speculations about its existence, and the impact finding it would have on history.

Then he told them about the phone call from Professor Bailey and the FBI's concerns that the Communists might also try to locate the ship wreckage with it's treasure. Chuck said he felt this was highly unlikely, but had heeded their warning to be careful about revealing his knowledge about the site location until they had left on the expedition. He apologized for not being completely truthful earlier.

That said, he passed out copies of a sketch of what he thought the urn would look like and said it was time to get back to business.

"The urn is probably 16 to 20 inches high, likely painted with script and characters about whose ashes are inside and it may be brightly colored," Chuck said. "Usually they had tops with knobs like this," he continued, pointing to his sketch.

"The burial urns of the period between 400 and 500BC were made from clay, hardened by baking at very high temperatures in a kiln. Much like it is done today. According to what I've learned, some of the earliest ceramic vessels that have been found were found in China. The urn we are looking for is likely made from a combination of bone ash and clay."

Will raised his hand. Chuck nodded in recognition. "Is that where the term, 'bone china' comes from?"

"In a way," Chuck continued. "Bone China, as we know it, first made in the West and perfected by the British in the late 16th century, was an imitation of Chinese bone china or as it is sometimes called, porcelain. But we're getting off the subject The important thing to remember, is that the urn, although somewhat hard, will still be easily breakable. The sketch you have should help. The best bet is to call Bryan, Karen or me if you uncover any kind of pottery and let us help you remove it. Any more questions about the urn or our expedition?"

There was some additional discussion, but in a few minutes all agreed it was time to call it a day.

Maria said she needed to call her mom.

Bryan had to call his wife and Jason said he had to touch base with his editor.

Of these three, one had already known about the urn, but not about the latitude/longitude readings that could precisely pinpoint the location of the wreck some 1,500 years before.

****

The phone rang in John Yang's room at the Gray Gull in Ocean Shores at about 8:34 PM.

"Hello," he answered tentatively.

"Is Mr. Tinkers there?"

This was the prearranged signal.

Yang responded, "There is no Mr. Tinkers here, only Mr. Chance."

That was the correct response. On the other end of the line, there was a noticeable sigh of relief. "You're late," said Yang. "I hope you have something of interest to report."

"Yes, I believe I do".

Chapter Nine

Southeast of Aberdeen, Washington, where the Chehalis river flows into Gray's Harbor is the town of Cosmopolis. It was here that the Monrovia was positioning itself to take on its cargo of wood chips from the Weyerhauser Mill the following morning.

Woo Xinghai had just finished talking to John Yang and was busy in the radio room writing out a message for transmission to Beijing. He was taking great pains to make sure the message was correctly coded and quickly transmitted to Beijing where it was Tuesday morning. He would wait for a response and then, at the prearranged time, contact Yang with further instructions for him and his agent with the search party. He knew that news of Coolridge's knowledge of the urn and navigational fix would accelerate their plans and he needed Beijing's instructions quickly if they were to have any chance of success. Woo had already told Captain Varney to be ready to leave port in the morning. He had also obtained agreement from the captain to use one of their ship's launches and two of the crew when the time came for action.

Woo shifted his heavy bulk in the chair. At forty-five he had been on many missions for his government, but this could be the most exciting yet.

Like John Yang, he had found work many years ago in the export/import business. Currently he worked for Ching Sen Food Products in Los Angeles. Unlike Yang, he had sought and obtained U.S. citizenship, but maintained his Nationalist Chinese citizenship as well. The dual citizenship afforded him many opportunities to travel to and from Taiwan. He had been able, over the years, to rise to the position of senior agent for the western United States. So far his ties to the People's Republic went unsuspected. This current mission was important, but being actively involved put him in a position of risk that he had not experienced in some time.

****

Chuck's search party had gotten a head start and crossed Ellen Creek at about 7:15 a.m. heading for a rock formation called *Sea Stack*, about a mile ahead. When the tide is out, it's a fairly easy hike. At high tide you are forced to climb over driftwood and contend with barnacle covered rocks. Some of the areas Chuck had assigned for investigation were not reachable at high tide.

Chuck and Karen walked at an easy gait with Jason keeping up for now. Chuck carried the sextant and the charts. Before leaving Seattle, he practiced taking sun shots and got some help learning how to use the instrument from a friend in the

Civil Engineering Department at the university. Fortunately, it was sunny, so far. Karen carried the metal detector and Jason had a pack with maps and their lunch.

"Karen, I can see Sea Stack rock up ahead. I want to shoot one or two sun lines there, then I'll take some when we get around Cape Johnson in another hour."

He would have to take some sun shots at noon, as well. If he did everything right and the sun cooperated, he should have their precise location. Tomorrow he would take more readings when they got closer to the Norwegian Memorial.

"What is the map location you think was recorded again? I can't remember exactly from last night" asked Jason.

"As best I can tell, 124 degrees - 41 minutes West by 48 degrees - 1 minute North," Chuck answered.

Chuck explained that the kind of navigational equipment and charts they had 1,500 years ago were probably pretty accurate. After all, they did come all the way up north, sail west and then down the Alaskan and Canadian coasts and even further before they headed back.

"They appear to have kept good logs."

"Didn't they have sextants back then?" Jason asked.

"No. Sextants weren't used until the 18th century. We know that ancient navigators used the stars and sun to guide them much as we do today. They may have had some type of crude sextant, but we don't know for sure."

****

The other two teams were a few minutes behind Chuck's party and were nearing the huge rock formation called Sea Stack.

"Chuck said we should start looking along the cliffs and headlands when we go past Cape Johnson," said Maria. Turning to Jerry she asked, "What's that, about another mile?"

"About one and a half," answered Jerry, giving Maria his best smile.

It was an unusually bright sunny day and the two were enjoying each other's company. Jerry had earlier apologized for not being forthcoming about the 1966 incident, but Maria had said she understood and hoped they would discover something that might be helpful in solving the mystery.

"So what are we looking for exactly, I mean as far as the Chinese thing is concerned," he asked, shifting the conversation away from Dave Peterson.

Maria looked at Jerry and thought to herself. This guy's really nice. I wonder why he's not married? Then, having paused too long, she tried to answer his question.

"Well, as Chuck said, with all the storms, normal erosion and the passage of time, the only thing that makes sense, if the chests are still here, is that they are in some cave or tunnel on one of the hillsides. Maybe covered up by accident, normal land movement or maybe on purpose to hide the location. There have been many slides around here over the last five hundred years. I'm sure there were back then too."

"Anyway," she continued, "We're supposed to look for openings to caves and tunnels on the banks and hillsides, especially those fairly high up and use our metal detectors as much as possible."

"Bill and I looked in several caves in '66, but never found anything interesting, even remotely. Bill's been over the area many times since. I suppose things change, and I do enjoy spending time with you," he added reaching out to touch her arm.

She smiled and acknowledged his touch. "You do, huh. All right, here's the Cape. It's time to start exploring."

****

The second team was just behind Maria and Jerry. As had been planned, they continued on for another half mile and started their search of the banks and coves off Sea Lion Rock.

"Here's where we're supposed to start," said Will. "Let's stay as close to each other as we can. Climbing around these rocks and into and out of these coves can be dangerous."

As the day wore on each team was meticulous, but found nothing of interest.

Chuck went just ahead of the Sea Lion Rock area and took some more readings. It was hard to do by himself, but he preferred it that way.

He spread the altitude correction tables out on a large, flat rock and with stop watch in hand, took the reading that would give him his first line of position.

He double-checked the column in the correction table for April-September, reset his stop watch and took a second reading. Now he had two lines of position. Enough for a dead reckoning fix.

With the new position plot in hand, Chuck rejoined Karen and Jason who had just caught up to him.

"How'd you do?' asked Karen.

"Fine. I'm sure we're not far enough north yet, but I want

to continue with our plans for now. Let's get a little closer to the edge of the cliffs and start working back south to join the others."

****

It was Karen who first spotted the rock carvings.
"Chuck, Jason, look at these," she said excitedly.
"What are they," asked Jason.
"They're called petroglyphs," Karen answered. "I first saw some of these up at Ozette. The early Indians carved the pictures as a way of telling a story or recording a special event. Much of the symbolism in this region has to do with fertility."
"Look," said Chuck pointing, "This one is definitely a whale, this one looks like a star and this one, oh, I see what you mean Karen."
Karen blushed a little as Chuck pointed out the petroglyph that was unmistakably part of the female anatomy. She was more embarrassed with Jason present, but he seemed distracted.
Just then Jason interrupted, "Hey, the tides coming in fast."
Chuck agreed and they climbed down from the rock they'd been on. Chuck asked Jason to find the other teams and to let everyone know they'd be heading back to Rialto Beach in about an hour. He hadn't really expected to find anything today, but wanted to make sure and wanted to hear their reports. Tomorrow, Chuck intended to rise at dawn and hike to the Norwegian Memorial to take more navigational readings. The teams would begin at the spot where he and Karen had started and continue north, unless they had not

finished their search area today.

Everyone got back to camp about the same time and Chuck held a short debriefing before dinner. Bill and Willis had found several cliff openings and a small cave that proved to be of no significance. Chuck and Jerry reported likewise. Karen told them about the petroglyphs she found and explained about the origin of the rock carving to those in the group that had never heard of them. Then Chuck asked for everyone's attention.

"I took several sun line position shots today and I'm pretty sure that the sight is closer to the Memorial, but thought we should still check south," said Chuck.

"Tonight after dinner we'll plan for tomorrow. Will, Jerry says that you do a fine talk on Totems. I hope you'll give us a little campfire program tonight. It can't hurt to get a little culture and learn about the Makah."

"Sure, I'd be happy to," said Will.

"So, let's break for now. We've got about an hour before dinner," said Chuck.

This night it was Bill and Maria's turn to fix dinner. They served Sloppy Joe's, a green salad and corn-on-the-cob.

Everyone seemed to enjoy the meal. Chuck passed the word that they would have a meeting again about 7, followed by the campfire. Several asked about what time the campfire would be over because they wanted to call home. Chuck said he figured about 8:30.

Everyone had their turn at reporting anything additional they had observed that day and then Chuck went over some of his notes and made adjustments necessary for the teams to get started early again in the morning. "All right," Chuck concluded, we all have our assignments for tomorrow. Jason will stay here and Bryan will join Will and Bill's team. My

Sextant readings will likely confirm the area around the Norwegian Memorial, give or take a minute or two, is our best bet, but I still want you to begin where you left off yesterday and work northward.
Any more questions?" No one spoke. He turned to Will.
"So, Will, how about some totem lore before we all turn in," Chuck said, relieved to be turning the meeting over to someone else.

****

"The totem figures, like the Orca whale, do not represent the animal, per se, but the form that an ancestor took in some mythical time. Significant events are illustrated, such as floods or earthquakes or special visitations by other tribes."
Will told them how his family's totem was in his mother's home in Neah Bay and how visitors always commented on its uniqueness when it was brought out for big get-togethers which the Indians called potlatches.
"So what's so unique about your totem, Will," asked Maria.
"To start with, it's only about 6 feet tall, a bit shorter than the average. It has five distinct symbols. Three are fairly easy to figure out: a whale, an eagle and a bear. The fourth looks like a face with three eyes and that gets me a lot of kidding. Some say that maybe some alien visited my ancestors in another life. But it's the fifth that's really odd. The carving looks like it's supposed to be four flat boxes on top of each other with flags sticking out of the top box. Real strange, too. The sides of the flat sections have small circles carved into

them. Over the years my family has gotten many odd comments about its totem."

****

John Yang's room at the Gray Gull Motel was on the third floor and on the street side, so he had no view of the water. Perhaps it would have soothed his nerves if he had. The agent with Coolridge's group was late again in reporting. John's stomach was doing flip-flops.

His dinner at Mariah's Restaurant next door to the motel had been excellent, but he'd eaten too much, too fast. The phone finally rang and after the customary passwords, Yang spoke first.

"You are late again."

The agent from Mora campground responded.

"We are going to have to change the time to 9 o'clock, 8:30 is too early. It looks like I just can't get away before 8:30 or 8:45. Anyway, I have nothing of significance to report. The teams searched the area as planned, but nothing was uncovered. I feel strongly that tomorrow will be a more productive day. I suggest you tell the ship to delay heading north as long as possible and prepare to initiate the plan early the following morning. I will call tomorrow night at 9 to confirm."

Yang didn't like being dictated to, but it appeared his agent was on top of the situation.

"All right, you are in the best position to know. I will be ready for your call tomorrow night. He almost added, "and please be prompt," but thought better of it. It did sound like the agent was on edge and Yang didn't want to add any more pressure.

****

Two of the prime reasons the U.S. Coast Guard keeps a close watch along the western Washington coast is to discourage drug trafficking and to keep Russian ships from gathering information about atomic submarines. In 1981, the Cold War was still tense. Monitoring for spy ships was a top priority. The only path to the ocean for the US subs stationed in Hood Canal is north, through the Strait of Juan de Fuca, and then out past Neah Bay into the Pacific.

The Hood Canal waterway separates the Kitsap Peninsula from the Olympic Peninsula. Sub Base Bangor and the Underwater Warfare Base at Keyport are located in Hood Canal.

Although drug trafficking was a concern, electronic surveillance by foreign vessels got more emphasis. Some Russian ships sailed as close to U.S. waters as they could to conduct electronic spying. The United States had several listening stations along the coast and the Coast Guard closely monitored all communications making certain Russian ships stayed in international waters. Russian subs also prowled the coast.

"Sir, this is seaman Bishop. Lt. Mason asked me to call and report that for the last two nights we have picked up ship to shore communications from somewhere in Ocean Shores to a Liberian ship at the Port of Gray's Harbor. A few minutes after each call, the ship transmitted a message in Morse code.

It doesn't seem to be in English, either."

There was a pause and the commander asked a question.

"No, sir," Bishop answered. "We don't know if it's anything to be worried about, but Lt. Mason thought it odd that both calls were about 8:35 PM and the Morse message is not in any known language, so we assume it's in code. There's also been two calls around seven each morning on the same frequency."

"Yes Sir, we'll set up a tracker in Ocean Shores tomorrow night and see if we can pinpoint the sender's location. Yes, I understand, thank you sir."

Seaman Bishop turned to Lt. Mason. "The Commander said that they would check out the ship and see what its manifest and destination are, just to make sure. It may be one of those spy ships, but the transmissions to our coast are unusual."

****

Jerry threw a couple more pieces of driftwood on the fire. It looked like a nice night and he was hoping to spend some time alone with Maria. After the campfire meeting she had left in a hurry. She had to make a phone call and would be back as soon as possible, she said. She seemed frustrated during dinner, but he chalked it up to having to prepare the meal and cleanup. He volunteered to help with the cleanup before the meeting, but she declined to accept the offer. He had seen Chuck and Karen walking toward the beach earlier and he liked the idea.

It was almost dark when Maria returned from the Ranger station.

"Sorry I took so long. My dad wanted to know all the details of our trip so far and then I tried to reach my department head, but he wasn't home," she said.

"How about a walk on the beach?" Jerry suggested, offering his hand.

"Sure, it's a nice night, but the clouds over the ocean don't bode well for tomorrow. You know the old adage, 'red sky at night, sailors delight, red sky in the morning, sailor take warning.'"

"Yes, I've heard that saying, but maybe the morning will be okay. I hope so for Chuck's sake so he can take his sun shots, and it's sure clear overhead," Jerry said.

Marie gazed at the sky. "Look, what's that streaking across the sky?"

"Where?"

"See, just above the horizon, heading up toward the Big Dipper."

Jerry followed her hand and then he saw it too.

"Maybe a comet," he ventured.

Then remembering something he'd heard on the radio.

"You know, NASA just launched Voyager 2. Maybe that's it."

"Isn't that going to Saturn?' Maria asked.

"Yes," Jerry said. He looked at her as she followed the path of the light.

She was beautiful and Jerry was having trouble taking his eyes off her. He squeezed her hand. "I hope we can be on the same search team every day."

"I enjoy your company too," she said. She squeezed his hand back and they continued their walk.

"What do you think about our chances of finding the urn?"

"I don't know, the gold coins are one thing, but finding a 2,000-year-old urn in one piece is something else."

The two smiled at each other and continued their walk in silence, each wondering where this friendship would lead after the expedition was over.

****

True to his word, Chuck rose early and hiked to the Memorial to take some sextant readings. The sky was clear now, but out over the sea the western horizon had a reddish, foreboding glow. He set up the sextant on his tripod and took several readings. The stopwatch had been his dad's. Karen had found it in an old jewelry box just before they left Seattle. Somehow it seemed fitting that he was using his dad's stopwatch. When Chuck ran track in high school, his dad had used the watch to time him at practices. It was his dad that had encouraged him to go on to college and then to pursue his interest in ancient history.

Chuck finished his sun shots. The results convinced him that the area of greatest potential for discovery lay somewhere a half mile either side of the site of the Norwegian memorial. The hike back took about an hour. He arrived during breakfast.

"Sit down and eat. You've been gone a long time," said Karen when Chuck appeared. "How did it go?"

"Well, I'm convinced that the Norwegian Memorial area is about as close as I can pinpoint their readings, but I still want to go with our plan."

"Can I join in later?" asked Jason, overhearing their conversation. "I hate to stay here and miss the action."

"We'll see," Chuck said, "but I really need you to watch the campsite today."

An hour later they were back at their assigned starting places near the memorial. This region of the beach was littered with giant boulders, covered with barnacles and surrounded with pools of water left by the receding tide.

The Norwegian Memorial was about 8 miles from their campsite. It was named for a stone marker memorializing the Norwegian bark *Prince Arthur* that floundered on a reef in 1903. It was recorded that the helmsman of the *Prince Arthur* mistook cabin lights on shore for the Tatoosh Island beacon that marks the entrance to the Strait of Juan De Fuca. Either way, the ship was too close to shore and broke up on the rocks. Only two men survived. The 18 who didn't, lie buried beneath the stone memorial.

By one o'clock, meticulous searching had brought the teams within about 30 yards from the path leading from the beach to the memorial. Chuck suggested a quick break for lunch.

"Let's hike to the memorial for our lunch break," Chuck said. "You can see it there on that bank," he continued, pointing up the path. The memorial was not on the beach, but about 100 feet inland on a small plateau among some trees.

When everyone was mostly finished eating, Chuck rose and called for their attention.

"From here on, let's be extra careful to inspect anything that looks like an opening and continue to use your metal detectors near any suspicious mounds. Also, keep your eyes on the tide. I don't want anyone caught in a cove. We've probably got another two hours, so finish up and let's go."

"Jeez," whispered Jerry to Maria. "What does he think we've been doing."

"Yes," she whispered back. " I don't know how we could be more thorough." And then with a softness, "Is this near where your friend disappeared?"

"Yeah. It's real eerie coming back even though I was here several times after with Bill."

Bill overheard, and added, "It makes me feel strange, too. Okay, you heard what the boss said, Will and Bryan, let's go, while we still have some daylight."

They finished lunch and started their search again. The procedures Chuck had recommended were slow but thorough. He was a history professor, not an archeologist, but with Karen's help they had shown the others a routine for digging and removing debris. The metal detectors helped, but a lot of the work was on the sloping banks above the beach. Footing was tricky.

The work was even more meticulous now. Every slight reading on the metal detectors got rapt attention. To break the monotony, Bryan asked Will some more about his native background.

"I was fascinated by your totem story last night Will. You really don't even look Indian," he said trying hard not to sound prejudiced.

Bryan continued hesitantly, "Maybe the totem is influenced by other branches of the family."

Will turned to Bryan with a smile on his face. "You don't have to be so coy about it Bryan and I'm not offended. Over the years there's been a lot of inter-tribal marriages and an equal number of marriages to Europeans and Orientals. Today, some Makah look Norwegian or Swedish." Will chuckled at his joke and then continued.

"In my case, I don't know of any non-Indian influences on the Grove side till the late 19th century when a Dane named Sam Peterson married my great-grandmother."

"Was he from around here?" asked Bryan fascinated and relieved that Will wasn't offended.

"Seattle, I think," answered Will. "From the Ballard district."

"I'm from Port Angeles and we have quite a few Peterson's there too," said Bryan.

Will shrugged his shoulders. "Well I'm not really sure about Seattle or Port Angeles, but Great-grandpa Sam and a man named Clarence Munn were Treasury Agents working in Port Townsend in 1890-91."

"Really. Why Port Townsend?"

"Port Townsend was a big port back then. The Treasury guys checked out the Chinese ships that came to port, looking for opium being smuggled to the opium dens in town."

"It sounds like dangerous work," Bryan said.

"It was. Sam eventually quit the Treasury Department and left Port Townsend in 1891. We're not too sure whether he returned to Seattle, however a few months later he settled in Neah Bay. There he met and married my great-grandmother Emily," Will said.

"So," Bryan said, like he'd solved the mystery, "Maybe your Grandfather Sam carved those odd symbols on the Totem."

"It sounds like an interesting idea, but if anyone did, it would have been my grandfather Mike. He was the carver in the family. However, I'm sure that the totem as it looks today was around long before great-grandpa Sam came on the scene."

"How can you be so sure?" Bryan said.

Before Will Grove could answer Bryan's question, the metal detector's buzz brought them back to the task at hand.

"Man, that's a strong reading, and getting stronger," said Bryan, moving up the short incline between some beached logs. He slipped on some kelp.

"Be careful," said Will, and followed right behind Bryan.

They started carefully digging around near the spot which gave the strongest reading which happened to be at the base of a high sand bank rising out of the beach near a large group of rocks. Several large pieces of driftwood stuck out of the sand and made the footing difficult.

"See anything yet?" Bryan asked.

"Not yet --- wait," Will paused, and then continued to brush sand and seaweed away from the base of one of the larger driftwood pieces. He turned around to face Bryan with a slight smile on his face.

"Just a bunch of rusty nails," he said holding several up to show Bryan. Must have been dumped here years ago or maybe someone was using them to make a raft or something. Anyway, no gold!"

They left the nails by the log and continued searching along the bank, but the detector didn't register anything out of the ordinary.

Bryan followed behind Will who was using the detector. "How about my question on the totem?" he called ahead to Will.

Will turned back to him. "Well, just north of here on the west side of Lake Ozette there are some petroglyphs on a large rock and one of those images is almost identical to one of the totem images. It definitely outdates Sam."

"Which image?" asked Bryan now with some frustration. He hated to admit it, but he was still not clear on the meaning of the petroglyphs.

"It was the image with the four square blocks with flags or feathers sticking out of it," said Will. "I was told by Grandpa Mike, that the petroglyphs are hundreds to thousands of years old. They were carved in the rocks by my ancestors either using stones and other sharp tools. The word petroglyph literally means *rock carving*. They represent an event in the past. Often deal with fertility. They've been found all over the world."

****

Progress was slow for the other two teams too and Chuck checked his watch, concerned about the tide. He caught Karen's attention.

"Karen, let's join in with Jerry and Maria, maybe we can move along faster." He yelled to Bryan to watch the tide. Bryan's team was just ahead of theirs. Bryan heard Chuck's warning. The sky was getting very ugly, he thought.

Will and Bryan had just rounded a hill that formed a point jutting out from the bank near the path to the Norwegian Memorial.

Bill had already climbed part way up the bank when Jerry and Maria joined Bryan's team. As Jerry watched Bill something caught his attention and he yelled.

"Hey Bill, look up there between those trees. That's an opening I don't remember seeing before."

Not waiting for a response, Jerry quickly left Maria's side and climbed up to join Bill.

"Be careful Jerry," Bill yelled as he moved past, but Jerry was almost now just short of the rock outcropping about 30 feet above the beach.

Jerry didn't take long in reporting. "It's definitely an opening to a cave as far as I can see. I don't have my flashlight. Bill, come on up the rest of the way."

Cave of Secrets

Bill scrambled up the bluff and handed his flashlight to Jerry. "Here," he said. "Can you see better now?"

Jerry, now aided by the flashlight, peered more intently into the three to four feet wide opening.

"Looks like the storm last week washed away some ---, My god! It looks like a skeleton, and those clothes, Damn! Bill, tell Bryan to call the others. This may not be the location of the treasure, but I think we just found Dave Peterson!"

Chuck, Karen and the others hurried over.

"Can you see anything else Jerry?"

"No, not without climbing in. I think we might need ropes and some more light to do that," said Jerry, by now almost through the opening.

"Jerry, it's getting dark and the tides coming in. I'm afraid we won't have enough time left today," Chuck yelled.

Jerry ignored him and disappeared into the cave. Sticking his head back out a minute later he cried triumphantly, "I made it!"

"I can see what are obviously more skeletons and there are several pieces of painted wood panels. We need to get inside Chuck. This may be what you're looking for."

"Jerry, Bill yelled, "Chuck's right about the tide. We need to get out of here soon."

Bill continued to make his case for leaving. "We can come back in the morning and we should call Sheriff Maxwell right away."

"Just one more look," Jerry said.

As he turned to walk back into the cave to get a closer look at his find, he heard a cracking sound and then his footing gave way.

Bill heard the sound too. "Jerry?" There was no answer.

"Jerry," he called again.

He seemed to be all right but couldn't move his left leg. Jerry groped around for Bill's flashlight. "Damn," he thought. He could see some light above. Then he heard Bill calling.

"Down here. Watch out, a section of the floor gave out."

Just then a beam of light shown. It looked to be several feet above him.

"You okay?" Bill asked.

"Yes, scrapped up some and I can't get my leg free. Can you lower another flashlight? I've lost yours."

By this time Chuck, Karen and all but Bryan had climbed up to join Bill. They shined their flashlights into the dark cave.

"Looks like just a few feet of the floor gave way," said Chuck. "See, there's the other side."

"Chuck, give me your flashlight," said Bill.

Bill tied it to some rope and using Karen's light to guide him, lowered the flashlight.

"Shall I try to get down there," Bill hollered.

"No, I'm okay. I think I can move these rocks by myself."

And shortly he had. The rocks were not too large, but a dozen or so had ended up on his leg.

"Can you stand?" Chuck asked.

"I think so." Jerry was in a fifteen-foot deep hole, about 3 to 4 feet round. The rest of the floor seemed to be solid and none of the area with the skeletons was disturbed as it lay several more feet further inside the cave opening. There were still two or three feet either side of the edge of the hole that left a path.

"Grab hold of the rope," Bill said. With some effort, they pulled him up and out.

He had several cuts and scrapes and what was likely a twisted ankle, but was otherwise okay. Using one of their first aid kits, Maria and Karen attended to his wounds.

"Ouch."

"Sorry," said Maria. She wetted a rag and washed the dust from his face.

"There, you look like your handsome self again."

Jerry smiled and winked at her.

"Give me a hand Bill," Jerry said. With a noticeable grimace, he rose.

Bryan now joined the group. "How's he doing?"

"Fine, considering," said Chuck.

"Chuck, the tide is really coming in fast and if we don't leave pretty soon, we'll be stuck till daylight," Bryan said. The rest of the team heard his warning.

Bill left Jerry and went to where Bryan was standing just outside the entrance. "He's right Chuck, we've got to get out of here now. From what I see, we'll be trapped in another fifteen minutes or so." Bill continued.

"We can come back here in the morning and anyway, we should call Sheriff Maxwell right away before we disturb anything more in the cave."

Leaning on Will's arm, Jerry now was out of the cave, but he was noticeably limping. Karen had wrapped his ankle, but walking was still painful.

"But what if the rain from that storm out there causes another slide. And shouldn't we lay something over that hole," Jerry said.

Chuck turned to Jerry. "I know, but I don't think it's going to be that bad of a storm. We can mark this spot real good, then tomorrow we'll have everyone's help and lots of time."

"I disagree," said Jerry. "I think it's important someone stay here overnight. Now that we've found this spot it doesn't make sense to leave it unattended, regardless of whether there's gold inside. There's a campsite just over that bluff," he said, pointing back over his shoulder toward the cave entrance.

"Besides, my ankle's pretty bunged up and I'm not too sure I could make it back. I'll stay here tonight," Jerry said.

"I see Jerry's point," said Bill. "In fact, we ought to move our headquarters here first thing in the morning. One of us can wait for the Sheriff, while the rest pack up and move our gear."

Having the campsite closer to their discovery made sense to Chuck. "Okay, you win. Let's gather whatever we can for Jerry to spend the night and get started back before we're trapped by the tide."

Then to Will and Bryan. "Get some of those larger pieces of driftwood and cover the hole so we won't have to worry about that in the morning."

****

The clearing above them had three small campsites and one outhouse, and there was a water faucet. Also a previous camper had built a lean-to shelter that looked to be in good shape except for a few holes in the roof. Everyone helped to patch the gaps in the lean-to's roof. They left Jerry some food and a couple of blankets that Chuck kept in an emergency pack and headed south to Mora. Maria was the last to leave.

"Stay warm," she said. "I hope you won't be too lonely," she mocked playfully.

****

Chuck and Bill went together to the pay phone to call Sheriff Maxwell as soon as they got back. First they tried the home phone number Chuck had, but Maxwell's wife said he was still at work. Bill had that number, so he placed the second call.

It was just after seven and Maxwell was about to head for home when the phone rang.

"Hello, Maxwell speaking."

"Sheriff, this is Bill Jenkins, sorry to call you so late, but I think we've found Dave Peterson's body and maybe the treasure Coolridge has been looking for. Chuck's here with me now."

"Jesus, after all these years. I can't believe it," said Maxwell

"Can you come to meet us tomorrow?" Bill asked. "Chuck figures we'll need help too if the gold is there."

"Let's see," Maxwell thought out loud. "Tomorrow's Thursday, yeah, I'll get Frank Lakefield, the Coroner's assistant to come with me. I've already posted him on the possibility. Where can we meet you?"

Bill explained their location and they discussed possible ways to get there from Forks. Sheriff Maxwell said there was a Forest Service road that ran close to the Memorial, but that there'd been a mudslide and the road was blocked.

"I guess we'll have to drive the regular road and meet you at Mora," Maxwell said.

"That sounds right, but remember, you're not going to be able to drive past Rialto Beach so whatever you bring you'll have to pack on the hike up the beach trail," Bill reminded him.

"About how far?"

"The site is about 7 miles north of Rialto, near the Norwegian Memorial. Best bet is for me to meet you at the Ranger station. That's where I'm calling from and then we'll hike the beach trail."

Bill paused and Maxwell could hear him talking to Coolridge. He came back on the line.

"Chuck says the rest of the team will leave early. Jerry Helspath is spending the night at a campsite just over the hill from the cave entrance. Also, to remember that we'll need to transport some remains."

"All right," Maxwell said. "We should be there about eight, no later. I just can't believe it, we combed that area several times back in '66."

"I know," Bill said. "So did I, and many times since. See you in the morning."

****

When Bill and Chuck returned from the Ranger station the rest of the team was eating a meal hurriedly prepared by Bryan and Jason. Jason was voicing his displeasure at not being part of the discovery and asking questions as fast as he could of Will, Bryan and Maria.

"So," he asked Will and Maria, "you actually saw into the cave."

"Yes. Jerry saw more than we did but from what little we saw, there was definitely human remains and we think the one skeleton nearest the entrance is Dave Peterson," Karen said.

"He also saw some kind of broken wooden crates that Chuck thinks could be the ancient Chinese chests," said Maria.

"We'll all know for sure in the morning," Bryan chimed in.

He went on to explain about Jerry's fall and their reasons for the hasty departure.

Just then Chuck hollered, "Okay you guys, finish cleaning up and let's get together in fifteen minutes to plan our departure in the morning and talk through what we are going to do tomorrow."

"Bill, did you and Chuck get a hold of the Sheriff?" asked Will.

"Yes. He and a guy from the Coroner's office will be here in the morning. I'm going to wait for them at the ranger station and then follow right after you guys," answered Bill.

Bill continued, turning to Chuck, "Are we going to leave someone here tomorrow or are we all going to go to the cave site?"

"Tomorrow we all go. I think everyone will be needed," Chuck answered. Then, turning to Jason, "That should make you happy."

****

Ben Maxwell had been Sheriff of Clallam County for almost sixteen years. He was seriously considering whether to run again for another term. The Dave Peterson disappearance happened during his first term and he had always regretted not solving the mystery. Now, sixteen years later, it looked like his long wait was over.

He and Frank Lakefield had known each other since they both returned from the Korean War. Frank was one year his junior at fifty-seven. He looked a lot younger. Unlike Ben whose hair had turned almost white by the time he was fifty, Frank's hair was still dark brown. Lakefield answered on the second ring.

"Hello."

"Frank, it's Ben. They found Dave Peterson!"

"You're kidding. Wow! Okay, I suppose that means I'd better pack a bag," he said.

Chapter Ten

The sun had set an hour before and John Yang was starting to wonder if the phone would ever ring. The waiting was tedious and he wished he were more in the middle of the action rather than sitting around in the motel. It was 8:45.

John jumped from his chair when at last the phone rang just before 9 p.m. Without going through the password sequence, he immediately opened the conversation, trying to hold back his frustration.

The caller hesitated and then went ahead, also ignoring the password routine.

"Yes, John, I have good news to report."

"Go on, go on!"

"A cave has been found near the site of the ancient wreck. There are skeletons and parts of wooden crates or perhaps the missing chests."

"Excellent, did anyone see gold coins or an urn?" Yang asked expectantly.

"No there wasn't enough time to use the metal detectors or search anymore. The tide was rising and it was getting dark."

The agent explained about the plans for Thursday morning and the complications of the sheriff coming to the site, probably no later than 10 o'clock, plus Helspath's campsite above the bluff.

"Can you see the cave entrance from Helspath's camp?" Yang asked.

"I'm not sure," the agent answered, "but I don't think so."

There was a lull in the conversation while Yang thought.

"Can you get away tonight or sometime before dawn to meet the men from the ship?"

There was a pause.

"I don't know. I'm not so sure I could find the place in the dark and we'd need some good lights for inside the cave."

"But we must get in there before they do and lights are not a problem," said Yang.

The conversation waned again as the agent with the expedition pondered for a moment.

"All right, tell the ship I will be on the beach at 3 a.m. and will signal with three blinks of my flashlight. The men in the launch from the ship must have rope, lanterns and containers for any treasure we find and we must get in and out before we are discovered and I am found out."

"How will you get away undetected?" Yang asked.

****

On the ship, agent Woo related the news to the captain. The S S Monrovia pulled anchor and headed north. Then Woo readied the message to be transmitted to Beijing. He was sure the news would be celebrated.

Cave of Secrets

Next, he briefed the two crewmen who would go with him. He had decided the mission was too important for him to remain on the vessel while the launch went ashore.

****

In Ocean Shores, three men in an unmarked van electronically monitored on the frequency. They had about given up when they got the signal about 9 p.m.
"Call Lt. Mason, we've got a definite fix near the beach, probably at or near the Gray Gull Motel."
Their unmarked military van was parked in the center of Ocean Shores.
Mason answered.
"Mason here, yes, good and it looks like the ship is pulling out of port. Stay where you are for now and I'll call you back," he added.
Lt. Mason then called Commander Phil Farnsworth at the Coast Guard Station in Neah Bay. The options were discussed and then Farnsworth set a plan in motion. They would shadow the ship and await developments. Farnsworth told Lt. Mason to have the van move to the Gray Gull parking lot and to keep monitoring for additional communications.
Fifteen minutes later, Lt. Mason called Farnsworth again.
"Hello, Farnsworth. Yes, you say the ship is heading north? I would have thought it would be heading out to sea. Okay, keep me informed."

****

By 10 o'clock the campsite at Mora was quiet. Everything had been readied for the morning departure and everyone had turned in for a good night's sleep, except two of the team who separately stole away and headed north on the beach trail toward the cave and Jerry's campsite. One followed the other. The sky had cleared. The moon was almost hidden behind the two large rock formations off shore and it cast strange shadows on the beach.

Out of the shadows, the beach was brightly illuminated. The fir and cedar trees along the edge of the cliffs swayed gently. An owl hooted and then silently watched the two shapes below. The person behind was careful to stay back, avoiding detection.

****

Although he had been left snacks, Jerry hadn't been all that hungry earlier. Now, still awake at midnight, his stomach was growling and his leg ached. The thunder and lightning in the distance signaled an approaching storm. He was trying to decide whether to get up and rekindle the fire and have a snack when he heard the noise of someone approaching.

He called out. "Hello, who's out there?"

"Jerry, it's me," a female voice answered.

He recognized her voice and answered, "Over here, Maria."

"What the heck are you doing here at this hour? I'm surprised you could even find your way back."

"The moonlight helped, plus a good flashlight came in handy."

She turned back toward the beach momentarily, then turned back.

"Look's like a storm coming," she said. "Just thought you might like some company. I brought some food and a sleeping bag in case you get cold. Plus, I thought you'd need some help in the morning."

"Does Chuck know?" Jerry asked her.

"Sure," she lied, turning her face slightly, sensing his concern.

Jerry relaxed.

"The company is welcome and I can't get to sleep anyway. I can't think of anyone I'd rather be with tonight. I'm glad you came. We may get a little wet, though, it looks like the storm that's been sitting out there all day is going to finally come ashore."

"Well," Maria said, "I guess we'll just have to cuddle up to stay dry and warm, unless you have any objections. I know you're injured," she added with a sly grin.

"No, no objections. Quite the contrary," he said pulling her into the shadow of the lean-to shelter. Whatever restraint they had shown earlier, quickly evaporated.

****

The Monrovia moved slowly up the coast, making sure to stay just outside the three-mile limit. It was nearing 2 a.m. and Captain Varney estimated they would be in position to put the small launch in at about 2:30. His mate approached.

"Captain, we're getting some indication that another vessel is following. It could be a coincidence, but odd at this time of the morning. Radar shows quite a bit of rain ahead and we might be in for some rough seas."

"Keep me informed if the ship behind us stays on our heading or gets any closer," he answered.

He knew he had better advise Woo that they were possibly being followed.

Many voyages with too many nights in strange bars had left him feeling and looking well beyond his 52 years. His bulbous nose betrayed a love of rum and soda. His ever-increasing paunch added to the obvious look of bodily abuse. But the pay was good. These Chinese fellows had always delivered. But being shadowed by some other ship definitely had him bothered. Probably just coincidence.

Varney left his cabin and went forward to where Woo and the two crewmen were preparing the launch. Woo was having a difficult time talking to the two men. The Captain could see the frustration on Woo's face and hear it in his voice.

"Woo, we may have a ship following us and the weather is worsening north on our heading," Varney said.

Woo said something loudly in Chinese which Varney guessed was an expletive. "How much time left before we're at the departure point?" Woo asked.

"About 30 minutes," Varney answered.

****

It was nice and dry under the lean-to shelter, but Jerry had been restless until he finally dropped off at about 1 a.m., with Maria snuggled up close. By 2:30 he was sound asleep and didn't stir when Maria left. She walked toward the beach pulling her parka hood up to shield herself as much as she could from the rain which was starting to come down hard. She checked her flashlight to make sure it was still working and continued.

Meanwhile another member of Coolridge's group left a temporary shelter nearby and headed toward the beach too.

****

Woo and the two crewmen were now a mile from shore and the waves tossed them about and the rain pelted them. The sailors were well prepared and Woo regretted he had turned down the offer of rubber coveralls. Their small outboard motor struggled against the cross current and their progress had been slow.

"We should see the signal soon," he told them, more with gestures than words. He wasn't all together sure they understood. They were both Portuguese and spoke little English and definitely no Chinese. His Portuguese was faulty at best, but he had picked up a few more words since he boarded the ship. Just then Woo thought he saw three light flashes. He checked his watch, noting it was just 3 a.m. Looking toward shore again, he saw a repeat of the flashes and pointed them out to the crewman at the helm.

"Look there! Head toward those flashes."

The helmsman seemed to understand and turned the launch to head in that direction.

Woo pointed his own flashlight and flashed three times, acknowledging the signal. He did so again at regular intervals as the shoreline came into view.

The tide was out quite a ways and Woo could see as they came nearer that they would have to beach the launch rather than anchor, as planned. It would be tricky as it was obviously a rocky beach and what light they had showed the outline of several towering rocks near the water's edge.

The sound of the waves pounding against the rocks was almost deafening.

"Watch out for those rocks," he yelled back to the helmsman.

They were close enough now that Woo could just make out the outline of the agent who continued to flash the light as they neared the water's edge.

****

Jerry stirred as Maria slipped back into the warm space beside him. She had gone as quickly as she could to the crude outhouse at the campsite, trying not to get too wet. As she returned she noticed what looked to be someone out in the water with a light blinking off and on. Then she saw it again. She looked at her watch. *How strange at 3 o'clock in the morning,* she thought. She wondered if she should wake Jerry but her fatigue convinced her otherwise. He was sleeping so soundly, too. She'd tell him in the morning. She nuzzled up against him and fell fast asleep.

****

The US Coast Guard ship had been on the tail of the Monrovia for some time now and Lt. Simpson was keeping his base informed. Seaman Fletcher had advised him that the Monrovia's speed had slowed. Then just now that she appeared to have come to full stop. Time to call his base.

"Base, this is Simpson. Looks like she's stopping. What do you advise?" The answer came quickly.

"Let us know for sure if she remains stopped, but stay well away for now. We still have no justification to board at this time."

"Aye, aye," said Simpson. He relayed the message to Fletcher and the other seamen.

****

As he continued to flash the light, Jason Winslow wondered if this was really what he would end up doing when John Yang recruited him.

He met John Yang at a Seattle University Alumni banquet three years ago when he moved back to Seattle to take the job with the P-I. They both seemed to have the same ideas and philosophies and fast became good friends.

Eventually, John told him the story of his parent's persecution at the hands of the Nationalists. Jason was a good listener and sympathetic. He had never been to Mainland China, but had been to Taiwan and was shocked at the strong Military presence and the iron rule of Chiang.

Jason was also a strong critic of the government in the States and privately criticized his country for not supporting Communist China in its battle with Chiang and his government.

Yang of course fed on this and slowly bred Jason from a passive sympathizer to an active participant.

Jason's reporting job at the P-I was reasonably satisfying, but he was low in the pecking order, so from his point of view, the assignments were boring and his pay too low. After a year of grooming, John suggested Jason might be able to help the Communist Chinese with his writing and by gathering information for the cause. Winslow took the bait.

He was naïve at first, not making the connection that John Yang was actually working for the communists. Not just a sympathizer like himself. He had to admit, however, that the idea of being a "spy" intrigued him and added a little spice to his life.

So what could it hurt to pass on a few things he learned about Boeing's development projects. One story he was assigned took him to the sub base at Bangor. He wasn't allowed access to much of the base, but afterwards, Yang seemed excited about everything Jason reported seeing. He got an extra bonus that time. Eventually, Jason realized the obvious, but he was hooked. The money was intoxicating. Now this. He hadn't bargained for this. It really was like being a spy.

As he stood in the rain, he thought, *What if I'm caught? Am I really doing anything wrong by helping to return what rightfully belongs to China?*

No, he concluded, a stroke of luck and here he was on the beach in the middle of a grand adventure. Getting paid nicely for it too.

He knew he had to get to the spot on the beach to meet the boat, but he had wondered whether he would find the right spot. From everyone's talk he thought he could. Coolridge said they'd marked the location with stakes.

Then he spotted Maria sneaking off and took a chance following her. Sure enough, she had led him to the campsite where Jerry was. The rest was easy because Coolridge and the others had placed the stakes on the hill below the cave.

He had shined his light up the cliff and seen the opening. Then he'd found shelter and waited till it was time to signal.

****

The boat landed roughly and Woo and one crewman jumped out in ankle deep water.

Even though it was August, the water was very cold. The other crewman gathered their gear and passed it to the two men. He stayed with the boat while Woo and the other walked up the beach to meet the spy.

Jason had no trouble picking out Woo. He was, however, younger looking than he expected. Probably not much older than himself, he thought. Woo wore no hat, nor raingear, and the constant downpour ran quickly off his shaven head. Jason stepped forward.

"I'm Jason Winslow," Jason said, forgetting the password formality. "You are Mister Woo?"

"Yes," answering curtly. " Let's hurry, the tide will start going out soon. Lead the way. We only have an hour or so and then it will be difficult to get the boat in the water again."

Jason nodded, took some of the ropes and lanterns from the crewmen, and started walking toward the hillside. *Pretty good English*, he thought.

As they walked he asked, "Where's the ship? Will it be waiting for you?"

Woo answered as he hurried beside John. "They will stay out about 3 miles and return to our departing spot in about two hours, flashing the signal every 30 seconds."

Jason nodded as if he understood everything clearly, but he was still more than a little confused.

"Come, let's hurry," Woo added before Jason could say anything else.

The rain continued to pore down and it made it difficult to see, let alone climb a muddy slope with their gear. With some effort they made it up the incline to the rock outcropping at the cave's entrance.

"As you can see," Jason said, "the opening is only a few feet wide."

"Yes, I see."

"We'll have to be very careful going into the cave, there's a large hole just inside."

Jason went on to briefly explain what had happened to Jerry. Woo nodded.

Pointing to the Portuguese seaman, he said, "You, take this rope and climb into the opening." Woo explained as best he could to the seaman to watch out for the hole.

"You go next Mr. Winslow, and I will follow with the rest of our gear."

In a few minutes, they were all inside the cave. Their lanterns illuminated an eerie scene.

First was the skeleton of a person dressed in modern clothes. Jason explained to Woo that this was likely Dave Peterson who had been missing since 1966. Near him was some of his gear and what appeared to be a rotting notebook and flashlight.

Then, scattered about were the skeletons of many people. By the look of their rotted dress, these were the remains of the Chinese from the shipwreck almost 1500 years before. Near several of the skeletons were sections of what had likely been the wooden chests.

"I count at least twelve separate skulls," said Jason.

"Never mind that," said Woo. "Let's focus on finding the coins and the urn."

"Coolridge's team has metal detectors," said Jason as they started digging around the area near the wooden pieces they assumed were parts of the chests.

"So they do," said Woo, "but we should be able to find what we're looking for if we concentrate on this area."

The layers of dust and decaying vegetation on the cave floor was several inches thick, but more of the pieces of wood were visible as the first layer was removed. At first inspection there looked to be only matching parts for two large chests.

They started digging deeper around the wood panels and soon found part of what they had been hoping to find.

"Look," yelled Jason, "gold coins." In a few minutes he and the crewman found about 50 coins. Jason had no gloves and his hands quickly showed of his labors.

There was, however, no sign of the urn. There were parts of what had been a smaller box or chest that didn't have any gold around it. It was mostly intact except the top was pulled back.

Woo felt around the area that had the smaller pieces and noticed that this wood was brightly painted, unlike the other larger pieces. He decided to ignore the wood pieces for the moment.

"Ouch." Woo held up a shard of pottery just a few inches long.

"What's that?" asked Jason

Woo didn't answer at first, but felt around some more.

"Give me some more light," he commanded.

Shortly, he found another piece like the first. The color was a deep blue, almost purple and you could just make out part of some script. Both Jason and Woo continued digging in the same area. No more shards were found.

Jason turned to Woo, "So do you think these pieces are from the urn?"

Woo didn't immediately answer, but tried to fit the two pieces together.

"They look like they could fit together. See they're not flat, but they're curved," Woo said.

Woo handed the pieces to Jason.

"I'm no expert, but these could be part of the top of the urn," Jason said, remembering Coolridge's sketch.

"And see, this one has what looks like part of a knob. They must be from the cover on top of the urn," Jason said, handing the pieces back to Woo.

"They could be," said Woo, "but let's keep looking."

In a half hour they had cleared most of the debris away and were loading the two sacks Woo had brought with coins, but still no urn or more parts from what they now speculated had been the top of the urn. The going was slow. They had no metal detector. All they could do was dig around and sift through the debris in the dim light. Jason remembered reading somewhere that metal detectors didn't register pure gold, so a detector might not have done them any good, anyway, if the coins were 100% gold.

"What do you want to do, Mr. Woo?" asked Jason after another half-hour had passed. It was obvious that the urn, if it had been there at all, was either gone, or buried deeper than they had searched.

At this point the Portuguese crewman attempted to communicate to Woo that it was getting light out and that the tide was likely quite far out. Jason silently echoed the same fears. Woo nodded.

"I guess we must go. We will have to leave what coins we haven't found. I'm not sure we can even carry what we have found to the boat. Besides, I'd guess we only have another 30 minutes to get to the boat and head back out."

"The urn is another question," pondered Woo.

"Yes," said Jason, "but it does appear this smaller box contained something other than gold. Whatever was in it may be gone except for the two shards."

"Perhaps it is still here." Woo suggested. Then with a look of resignation, he rose and started gathering up their gear.

When they finished packing, Woo turned to Jason.

"You, of course must also get back before they discover you are gone," Woo said.

"I'll take the two shards we found with me."

"You will stay with the others and if they do find the urn, get it away from them and contact John Yang. But I think it is gone. If these two pieces were part of it, it has been gone for some time. Now, we must be off. We will assume the urn is still here for now."

They hefted their loads and headed down the bank to the beach.

Jason helped them load the boat and helped push it out, which proved difficult. The tide had gone out farther than they had expected. He didn't anticipate a thank you and he didn't get one. Woo told him to quickly return and when he could, call Yang with a report.

It was almost 5 a.m. when Jason started back to the camp at Mora. He thought about Woo's last admonition. How would he, "get it away from them?"

****

Lt. Simpson kept his ship as close to the Monrovia as possible without giving himself away. It was dark and the rain clouds obscured whatever moonlight might have been. The lack of light helped shield him too. About two hours had elapsed. The darkness and rain had also obscured the launching of the small boat with Woo and the two men. When flashing lights were seen, it was difficult to see at first where they came from. Seaman McCoy had been the first to see the lights.

"Look, Sir, someone is flashing a light. See, three times, then a pause and it looks like three more."

"Yes, I see, it looks like it's between us and the shore. Probably signaling our mystery ship," said Lt. Simpson.

"What should we do now?" asked McCoy.

"Let's stay back and see what happens. It's probably a drug deal like the commander thought, but let's get as close as we can for now and keep watch. We're not picking up any electronic signals so I think we can rule out spying."

****

The going was tough against the ever-increasing size of the waves. The launch with Woo and the two men made little progress toward the rendezvous.

Woo sat at the center of the launch straddling the two sacks of coins. "Can't you go any faster, it's almost 5 a.m. and fast getting light," Woo exclaimed.

The crewman, a man named DeParmo, or something like that Woo thought, shrugged his shoulders. The other, whose name was Manoel, fiddled with the outboard engine, but their speed didn't change.

Woo looked at his watch and decided that even though it wasn't yet 5:00 they should begin signaling. DeParmo took the flashlight. He had a difficult time using the flashlight and holding on at the same time. The height of the waves increased and they were constantly being pushed back toward shore and off course. DeParmo finished signaling for a second time just as a giant wave caught them broadside.

****

The Monrovia circled back at slow speed. Captain Varney reckoned that at 4:50 a.m. they were just about in the zone where they should meet the launch.

"Captain, the ship is still following us," reported the mate.

Varney thought to himself and then aloud, "Damn, it's probably the Coast Guard. I forgot about that. They probably think we're drug trafficking or spying on their subs."

The explanation now seemingly clear, he turned back to the mate.

"Any sign of Woo and the launch?"

"No, but it's still a few minutes before five o'clock."

"All right, proceed at slow speed and let's hope that if it is the Coast Guard, they won't try anything before Woo gets back."

Then, somewhat angrily, he added, "God, I hope they don't see the signals!"

"Have the radioman contact Yang in Ocean Shores. We will need direction if Woo doesn't make it back or we are boarded by the Coast Guard."

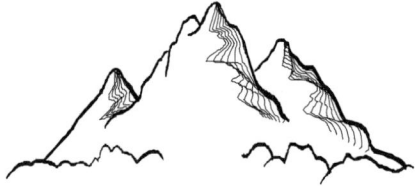

Chapter Eleven

Jessica Lancaster hated it when she had to come in early to relieve the night manager at the Gray Gull. Once a week was plenty. She especially didn't like the drive from her house on the point at 5:00 in the morning. This morning she had hardly been able to see her way through the thick fog. Last night on KIRO, she had heard it was supposed to be a nice day today. There were a few rays of sunlight peaking through to the east, so maybe the fog would burn off by noon. When she got to the reception desk, she noted a wake-up call scheduled at 5:20 for Room 209.

Banks of fog that settle over the beaches in the morning often hid sunrises on the Washington coast. Even in August, it is quite dark at 5:15 a.m.

John Yang was fast asleep with his wireless radio safely stored in the closet. The plan was for him to contact the ship at 5:30 a.m., so he'd set his alarm for 5:15 and left a wake-up call at the front desk for 5:20 as a back up. He had had a restless sleep worrying about today's events.

Several miles north at the Mora campground, Karen stirred in her sleeping bag. Turning, she noticed Maria was gone.

Probably gone to the outhouse, she thought.

Then she noticed the missing sleeping bag. At first she thought Maria had gotten up earlier and was packed and ready to go.

Chuck also began to wake. Seeing that it was getting light, he decided to dress and put on the coffeepot. The coals in last night's fire were still warm, so in a few minutes he heard the sound of boiling water.

By 5:45 a.m. Bryan and Will had risen. They joined Chuck at the fire and poured themselves some coffee.

"Thanks for the coffee," said Will. "I could smell it from the tent."

"You bet. Have you seen the others?" Chuck asked Bryan.

"Yeah, Bill's up and I thought I saw Karen heading for the outhouse, but I haven't seen Maria or Jason yet," said Bryan.

"Good morning, the coffee smells good," Karen said as she joined them a few minutes later.

"Good morning to you." Chuck rose to kiss her. "Any sign of Maria?"

"No, and I'm surprised, I thought she'd gone to the toilet, but she wasn't there and her pack's gone," said Karen, concerned.

"How about Jason?" asked Bill. "Did you see him? He's not in his tent either."

Karen turned and headed back to her tent to check again and start packing herself.

A few seconds later she stuck her head out and said, "Hey, all Maria's stuff's gone, but I found a note from her."

"What does it say?" said Chuck.

Karen read it to herself first and then a smile appeared on her face.

Cave of Secrets

"I should have known. She left last night and went to see Jerry."

"Jeez, I hope she made it okay."

"No pun intended," Karen said with a chuckle.

Bill, Will and Bryan laughed. Chuck didn't see the humor.

"Lighten up, Chuck," said Bill. Chuck continued to frown.

"Says she'll meet us at Jerry's campsite," said Karen, still smiling, ignoring Chuck's frown.

Chuck was in the midst of a minor tirade, when he spotted Jason approaching from the beach trail.

"And where have you been?"

"Just went for a walk," Jason said.

"It was a nice morning and the rain has let up. So what's all the fuss about?" he asked Will, avoiding Chuck for the moment.

As Jason turned away, Chuck noticed Jason's hands were quite dirty and he thought he saw some blood. *Must have fallen on the beach*, he thought.

"Maria's not here and we just found out she went to be with Jerry last night," Will said, "and Chuck's more than a little pissed."

"Okay, all right, that's it. Let's have a quick breakfast and get going," said Chuck. "I'll deal with Maria later."

****

John Yang had barely gotten the radio set hooked up when it rang.

"Yes," he answered, surprised because it had been arranged for him to call.

After the password exchange, the calling voice said, "This is the Monrovia, please hold for the Captain."

Varney came on the line. "Mr. Yang, we have a problem."

He explained the suspicioned presence of a Coast Guard ship and that Woo had not yet returned. He asked for advise and told Yang to call back in 15 minutes.

Just as Varney broke contact with John Yang, First Mate Ernst Jensen entered the radio room of the Monrovia and reported that they had seen signal flashes. He assumed it was Woo and the returning boat. He also reported that the wind had picked up and the sea was getting very choppy, so the launch would be bucking the wind and waves as they got father out to sea.

"Signal them back and when they get close try to tell them we're probably being followed," said the Captain.

Jensen left the room and returned the signal as instructed. Then he prepared to get the winches ready to raise the boat and the men back on board.

Just then Lt. Simpson hailed the Monrovia. Her decks were illuminated by the search light from the Coast Guard ship. The command was loud and clear.

"Vessel Monrovia, cut your engines and prepare to be boarded. This is the US Coast Guard cutter Franklin. Repeating, hold fast and stop your engines, this is Lt. Simpson of the US Coast Guard."

****

The launch seemed at first to hang on its' side, but then a second wave hit it and they were flipped over. As the launch came down, the motor propeller hit Manoel seated in the stern, killing him instantly. DeParmo, who had been seated forward of Woo, doing the signaling, ended up under the launch. He had not buckled his life jacket and now, in total darkness, he vainly tried to connect the ends. Woo was thrown clear of the launch. But something was wrong. He was being pulled under. He had his life jacket on, and like DeParmo, he had been careless about fastening the straps. In a panic he realized too late that the tie string from one of the coin bags was looped around his shoe. Desperately he struggled to unbind the strings, but the downward pull was too much. He was fighting a losing battle. He couldn't fasten the jacket straps and unbind the bag strings at the same time.

****

Welcoming a slight break in the weather, and unaware of the drama at sea, Chuck and the rest of the group approached Cape Johnson.

"What a great morning," said Will Grove. "I thought it would still be raining this morning, but it looks like a good day."

"Yes, it's great," said Bryan. "It should help Bill catch up with us soon."

The hillside along their path looked like a big green carpet that had been woven between the gray rocks and the spruce and hemlock trees. The vine maples, hip-high ferns and huckleberry bushes were still covered with dew and glistened in the sun. Then the hillside disappeared as it turned sharply inward where the ocean's waves had carved out a cove. The craggy walls of some coves often hid cave openings and tunnels.

Karen walked with Chuck, trying to get him to relax. "Come on Chuck, Maria's leaving to go see Jerry isn't going to cause any harm. She did leave a note and took all of her stuff. "Look what a beautiful day it's going to be."

Jason was walking with Bryan and Will and thinking to himself. *I hope Woo got back to the ship. I wonder if the urn is still in the cave or if it was ever there.* Then he remembered the shards. *Could they be part of the urn?* He almost said that out loud.

He wished he had had time to call John Yang, but Chuck had pushed everyone to get going.

"We should be there in another 10 to 15 minutes," Chuck said to everyone.

****

Jerry and Maria awoke about 6:00 and were finishing some dry cereal Maria had brought. It was still chilly and the fire felt good.

"So, do you think last night means it's forever?" she said.

"I don't know. I guess that's up to you," he said quietly.

"Why me? it's a two way deal you know," Maria said, sounding hurt. It had been only 3 days but she felt like she had known him a long time already. And after last night?

"There's more coffee," offered Jerry, changing the subject.

"No thanks," she answered. "Maybe we'd better clean up and get to the cave."

"What's the hurry?" Jerry asked. He was tightening the wrap on his ankle and putting a new Band-Aid on one of the cuts on his arm.

"It looks like the rain has stopped for a while. Maybe if we can do some clearing at the cave before Chuck gets here, he won't be mad at me," she said.

"Why should he be mad?" Jerry said in surprise. But he could tell by her expression that something was bothering her.

"I lied last night. I didn't tell anyone I was coming to see you," she said, lowering her face. "I did leave a note in the tent so Karen would see it, though. Sorry I lied."

Jerry put his arm around Maria.

"I'm glad you came. I'll go to bat for you with Chuck and besides, I'll tell him it was for medicinal purposes," he said with a grin.

"And, in answer to your question about last night, I'd like to think it means for ever."

Maria smiled. It was enough for now. "Let's finish cleaning and head down to the cave," she said. She gave him a peck on the cheek and gently slipped out from under his arm.

"How's the leg?"

****

Bill Jenkins was hoping Sheriff Maxwell would be early and he was pleased to see him pull into the Ranger Station parking lot about 7:30 a.m. Bill didn't recognize the passenger but assumed he was the guy from the coroner's office.

"Hello, Bill, good to see you again. This is Frank Lakefield; Frank, Bill Jenkins."

"Hi, nice to meet you," said Bill. "We had best get going. Chuck Coolridge and the rest have about a half hour start on us."

"Can I help with your gear?" Bill asked them both.

"No," said Lakefield, "but thanks."

As they hiked to the beach and then headed north, Bill and the Sheriff talked at length about the odds of finding Dave Peterson after all this time and then about the chances of finding Coolridge's Chinese treasure.

"Yeah," Maxwell said. "To think of all the people that must have gone near that cave, including our own search parties back in 1966, and no one found any sign of an opening."

"But remember," Bill said, "it's about 30 feet up. Until the rock and dirt were disturbed, you'd never know it was there."

"It was just luck that you spotted it," said Lakefield.

Bill noticed that both Lakefield and Maxwell were beginning to lag back and he slowed his pace.

Lakefield looked to be in good shape, but the Sheriff needed to shed a few pounds. He decided to stop for a minute.

"Maybe our group finding the cave was meant to be. We'll never know, but either way, Dave's fate is clear," said Bill.

"Perhaps it was the spirit of the Buddha in that Chinese urn that eventually lead the way," said Maxwell, none too seriously.

They all laughed, then Bill said, "You never know, do you."

Bill moved away from the large rock he had been leaning against. "Okay, we'd better get going."

****

Cave of Secrets

At sea, the captain of the Monrovia knew it was inevitable so he signaled the engine room for "All Stop" and thought about what he would say to the Coast Guard. He wasn't trafficking in drugs, had no unauthorized or illegal cargo, and no electronic listening devises. So other than being off his registered course, Varney couldn't see how he had broken any laws. *What about Woo and the launch,* the thought. *Should he tell them about it. Did they see the signaling?* He may have some explaining to do. He wished Woo were on board to consult and wondered why John Yang had not yet called back. Where was the launch?

****

At the Gray Gull, Yang had tried twice to raise someone on the ship and finally on the third try, the radioman answered. Without the prolog of passwords, Yang began speaking.

"This is Yang, get me Captain Varney."

"Just a minute, I will get him," responded the operator.

Varney was just outside the radio shack talking to First Mate Jensen. Quickly he followed the radioman.

"Yang," said the Captain a moment later. "Where have you been? We are about to be boarded by the Coast Guard."

"I have been formulating a plan. Is Woo on board yet?"

"No, but they may have spotted him. We've had no contact from the launch in a while, so perhaps they saw the Coast Guard ship and headed back to shore."

"So you have no idea whether they found the gold and the urn?" Yang asked.

"I have no idea," said the Captain. *What an idiot he thought. How would I know?*

"What are your instructions?"

"Listen, you have committed no illegal acts and you are outside the three mile limit. The problem will be to explain why you are heading north and about the launch if they saw it."

Yang told him one idea would be to claim that they were experiencing engine trouble and rudder problems. As far as Woo and the launch, Varney would have to improvise.

****

As soon as they got close to the cave, Jerry and Maria noticed that someone or something had been there since they had gone the previous afternoon.

"Look at all the foot prints and deep grooves in the sand. These had to have been made since we left, because it was nearing high tide," Jerry said. "Looks like two or maybe three different impressions."

"You know," Maria said, "I did notice some lights last night when I went to the outhouse, but I thought they were out in the water, not here on the beach."

"You wouldn't have seen any here, I don't think," Jerry said. "The high bank would have obscured this area from our camp site."

"So who would have been here?" pondered Maria.

"I don't know, but let's see if we can get closer to the cave opening. Did you bring the flashlight?" he asked.

"Yes, but shouldn't we wait till Chuck and the rest get here?"

"No, well maybe, but let's see if we can see anything. Besides, they should be here very soon," he added.

Their path the rest of the way up the side of the cliff was easier. The rain had stopped for some time. In just a minute, Jerry was near the ledge at the cave entrance. He shined his light in while making sure Maria had a good foothold near him.

"For sure someone's been here. The opening is definitely larger than it was yesterday and it looks like someone's been messing around inside And look, the branches we laid across the hole I fell in are moved too. I don't think we ought to go any further until the rest get here. The sheriff will want to check on things first," Jerry said.

He and Maria reluctantly climbed back down and waited for the rest of their party.

****

Captain Varney greeted Lt. Simpson warmly as he came abroad.

"Lieutenant, greetings," he said in broken English. "Sorry we are a bother and have been wandering around. You see we have been having engine trouble. It's fixed now."

Varney silently prayed John Yang's idea of a story would be convincing. His only problem now was if Woo and the launch were seen.

"Engine trouble, you say! Your manifest states you would head south from Gray's Harbor," Simpson said.

Captain Varney started to answer with excuses and more about engine and rudder trouble when Simpson interrupted him.

"Stop," said Lt. Simpson. "That's enough for now. I've been instructed to search this ship one way or the other. We believe you are not what you appear to be."

Miles Varney puffed up with a most indignant look. He acted very insulted.

"I, of course, object," Varney said. "To show my cooperation, however, I will certainly agree to your wishes."

Simpson nodded. "You and I and two of my men will start our search."

****

DeParmo was able to get two of his jacket straps connected and paddle out from under the launch. Then grabbing a line that was tied to the stern, pulled himself onto the overturned launch. By this time, however, the waves had pushed him some distance. He could just make out the lights of his ship. *Strange, it looks like there were two ships,* he thought. There were no signs of Manoel and Woo. He was very tired and cold.

Chapter Twelve

The skies slowly cleared. While Jerry and Maria waited they couldn't help marveling at the spectacular scene. The towering rock formations and the now gentle surf set a backdrop for the beach scene in front of them. The Gulls, Surf birds and the Sandpipers were feasting with the retreating tide. Two brown Pelicans flew overhead calling to each other.

The symphony of sounds made it hard to talk. Jerry decided to finish some toast from the morning and pulled it from his jacket pocket.

"Want a bite?" he said to Maria, showing her the toast wrapped in a napkin.

She shook her head.

"I wish we could just sit here together all day," Maria said, moving closer to Jerry on the log they were sitting on.

"Me too. What are we going to do when this is all over?"

Maria was silent.

A seagull perched on a nearby rock that was pockmarked with holes bored by Piddock clams. Next he cocked his head examining Jerry for any sign that food was in the offing.

Jerry tossed the gull a piece of toast. The bird snapped it up and flew off to another rock some distance away. Jerry turned to Maria.

"Kaloch to Seattle is a long trip for a date, isn't it," Jerry said.

Just then Maria spotted people in the distance walking their way from the south. Jerry slipped down from the log and helped Maria down.

"Here they come," said Jerry, now able to see that it was Chuck and the others on the beach.

Chuck, Karen, Will, Bryan and Jason were dragging after the eight-mile walk loaded down with the gear and equipment. Chuck took a sidelong glance at Jerry and Maria, and his face hardened.

"Thought you said in your note you'd meet us at Jerry's campsite," Chuck said looking directly at Maria. Then, disregarding Karen's earlier call for understanding, Chuck went over to Maria to confront her.

"Thanks. You were sure helpful this morning. I'm half tempted to send you back right now."

Jerry interceded. "All right Chuck, what's done is done, and we need all the help we can get. She's sorry, so let's say no harm done, okay?"

Before Chuck could respond, Jerry added, "Besides we've got bigger problems this morning."

"What's that," Chuck said, turning away from Maria.

"Somebody's been here since we left yesterday. Two, maybe three people and they were definitely up at the cave."

"Come on, let's get the supplies and gear up to my camp and I'll show you," Jerry said.

Chuck's expression changed but it was obvious, at least to Karen, that he was exchanging one tension for another. He had a passing thought about the FBI warning, but discarded it as highly unlikely. "I wonder," he said out loud.

"What's that, Chuck," Karen said.

"Oh, nothing." But she could sense that something was bothering him.

"Okay, Chuck said, let's go."

A few minutes later they gathered just below the rock outcropping and Jerry, Will and Chuck started to climb up to the cave entrance.

"Be careful Chuck, the ground's still a little slippery," Karen called.

In no time they were at the entrance to the cave.

"You're right, Jerry, someone's been here and by the looks of it they went into and out of the cave several times," said Will. "And look," Will said pointing to the ground, "that looks like a couple spots of dried blood on the rock near the entrance."

"It sure does," said Chuck.

"I'd like to go in right now, but I really think we should wait for the sheriff," said Chuck.

Below, Karen, Maria and Bryan were calling up questions and Jason was doing his best to act as surprised and upset as the rest.

"Do you really think someone was here?" Jason asked to no one in particular.

While they waited, they got most of the gear they would need up to a level spot near the cave opening. It wasn't long before they caught sight of Bill and two men coming up the beach.

"That must be Sheriff Maxwell on the right and that other

guy must be from the Coroner's office," said Chuck to Jerry.

"Yes, that's Maxwell and you're probably right about the other guy," Jerry answered.

Momentarily, the party of three joined them. Jerry, not wanting to wait, spoke first.

"Bill, Sheriff, someone or more likely several people were here last night after we left," Jerry said. He wondered if Chuck had told them about the FBI warning. But like Chuck, he decided that would just be too much of a coincidence.

"I can't believe it," said the Sheriff.

Bill stood still with a look of disbelief. "You've got to be kidding," he said.

Jerry continued, "No, unfortunately, I'm not."

"We haven't gone into the cave, but we should as soon as we can," said Chuck.

Chuck then said something to Jerry alone. Jerry nodded his head.

Turning back to the sheriff, Jerry went on. "Chuck suggests that you, Frank and I should get up there now and check the body we think is Peterson's."

The Sheriff nodded his head in agreement, then looked at Chuck.

"Chuck," said the Sheriff, "Frank and I know you're in charge of this expedition and we appreciate your patience. We'll be as quick as we can."

Chuck nodded and then Jerry, Sheriff Maxwell and Frank Lakefield climbed up to the cave entrance.

"Jerry, I notice you're limping, is that from your fall," said Maxwell. "Bill told us about that on our way here."

"It's better today, thanks," said Jerry. "But, be careful when you enter the cave, the hole is just inside."

****

Onboard the Monrovia, the search had just about finished. Lt. Simpson and his men had been thorough, but other than the cargo of wood chips there was nothing illegal to be found. No electronic listening equipment was discovered. Lt. Simpson was beginning to accept the Captain's story. He was in the midst of a conversation with Commander Farnsworth on shore.

"But what about all the calls we traced from Ocean Shores to the ship and the coded wireless messages that were sent just after?" Simpson said.

"I know," said Commander Farnsworth, "but just because someone sends them messages from the motel and they return messages, doesn't give us any reason to hold them."

He continued, "Lt. Mason and his men have pinpointed the Gray Gull and are now checking the registration for any clues, but, again, just sending messages isn't a crime."

"We'll try to figure out whose sending them and pass along the information to the FBI to check out, but we really don't have any jurisdiction there anyway," Farnsworth added.

"How about those flashing lights we saw?" Simpson asked. "If they were being signaled, maybe they had already finished sending something ashore."

Farnsworth thought about that and then told Simpson that if they couldn't prove it, there was nothing they could do. He would contact the local authorities and advise them that someone may have been smuggling in some goods.

"So, what should I do now?" asked Lt. Simpson.

Farnsworth replied, "If you're sure everything's on the up and up, I'd ask them to get going on their original course, follow them for a ways and then come back to port."

"Just to add emphasis, tell the Captain you're concerned about his engine problems and you'll follow him as far as Westport," he continued.

"I'm still suspicious," Simpson said, "but I guess you're right. I'll have the men make one more quick look see and then we'll apologize and do as you suggest."

****

During the search, Varney had kept quiet. It looked like they were in the clear and he was thankful, but impatient to call John Yang at the motel in Ocean Shores. And where were Woo and the two crewmen?

Simpson and his men were leaving the ship at last.

"Good luck on the rest of your voyage, Simpson called to Varney as he climbed over the side and proceeded down the rope ladder to his ship. And by the way, we will follow you back south, just to make sure everything is okay with your ship."

When Simpson got back on his vessel, he placed a call to Commander Farnsworth.

"Simpson to base, we're back on our ship and the Monrovia's headed south."

Chapter Thirteen

It was an eerie sight inside the cave when Frank Lakefield and Sheriff Maxwell climbed in and shined their lights. Jerry stayed just outside the entrance. After a few moments of dead silence, the assistant coroner spoke.

"Good God," said Lakefield, There's all sorts of skeletons in here. What a sight."

"Yeah," said Maxwell, "but I think this is Peterson for sure," pointing to the skeleton nearest the cave opening.

The skeleton was dressed in the clothes Jerry Helspath and Bill Jenkins had described to Maxwell some 15 years ago. They were amazingly preserved.

"Jeez," said Maxwell, "it looks like he was trapped in here and survived for a while. Look, here's what's left of a notebook. He must have written a message, but it's hard to read. The paper pretty well rotted away."

"Yes," said Lakefield, "it looks that way. He probably got in here and then something happened to cause the dirt and rocks to slide down and cover the entrance."

"No wonder Jerry and Bill missed him," the sheriff said. "They probably couldn't have heard him even if he shouted."

"Who knows, maybe he was temporarily knocked out," said Lakefield. "Anyway, it looks like it was an accident at first glance, but I'm going to have a closer look."

While Lakefield examined the skeleton they assumed was Peterson, Maxwell carefully picked up the notebook. After scrutinizing a couple of the notebook pages he said to Lakefield, "I think I can read a little of this."

He read out loud:

"----Batteries are about gone and matches ---, Jerry – sorry --- not your faul--- -f me tell my parents --- love them –

"Wow," said Lakefield, "What a way to go."

Lakefield stuck his head outside and called to Jerry.

"Jerry, pass that canvas bag into me," said Lakefield.

Jerry got the bag and handed it in. "How's it going?" he asked.

"Fine for now," answered Lakefield. "Shouldn't be more than a few more minutes."

Lakefield and Maxwell put all the bones and what was left of Dave Peterson's belongings into the bag and passed it out to Jerry.

"Ben," Lakefield said, "what about all the rest of this," pointing to the other skeletons and the scattered debris of wood pieces and clothing.

"What a mess. It's too bad, but I agree, someone's certainly been in here recently," Maxwell said surveying the rest of the cave.

"Looks to me like three sets of shoe prints, and one sure looks like a new pair of Nikes or Adidas, and look here there's a few spots of what looks like blood."

"It could be Helspath's blood," Lakefield said.

Cave of Secrets

"I didn't think he was back in this far," Maxwell answered.
"Anyway, it's time to let Coolridge and his team in here, but I suggest we stick around till tomorrow," the sheriff said to Lakefield. "Who knows what they may uncover!" Ben pulled out his camera and took several pictures.
"That should do it," he said.
They crawled out and told Jerry to tell Chuck and the rest that it was okay now to come into the cave.
Ben Maxwell turned to Jerry and motioned toward the body bag.
"We're pretty sure this is Peterson," he told him, "and we're going to stay around for a while, overnight if need be while you guys do your search in the cave." He repeated this to Chuck who had climbed up to their level.
Then turning back to Jerry. "I found part of what looks like Dave's journal of his last few hours of consciousness. I'll show it to you later. I think it will help you and Bill put all this behind you."
"Chuck, it's all yours for a while," said Maxwell.
"Didn't see any gold in there, but it looks like this is the spot you've been looking for," he offered as he and Lakefield made their way down to the beach with the bag.
Jerry, Chuck and Bill stayed above while Will and Bryan passed up more lanterns, a metal detector and more of their digging tools.
Chuck asked Maria to show Ben Maxwell and Frank Lakefield where the campsite on the bluff was so they could stow their gear and the body sack.
Jason turned to Chuck, "I'd like to go, too, I forgot my camera; it's in my pack."
"Okay." said Chuck, and then added, "Karen, I feel stupid, I should have brought our camera, too. Why don't you go with

them and get mine and while you're all there, set up a couple of the tents for tonight. But get back as soon as you can."

To reach the trail leading to the campsite, they had to cross over a series of puddles left by the retreating tide and the surrounding sand, still wet and soft.

Maria led the way with Jason and Karen close behind and Lakefield and Maxwell bringing up the rear. It took just a few minutes to get to the campsite.

Karen turned to Jason and Maria as soon as they got there. "Jason, you and Maria give me a hand." She started to say something to Maxwell, but Lakefield spoke first, anticipating what she intended to say.

"We'll set up ours over there," he pointed, "and then we'll give you guys a hand."

They moved a few yards away and when they were alone, Lakefield put his finger to his lips to signal Maxwell.

"Ben," he said quietly, "remember those footprints we saw at the cave entrance?"

Maxwell nodded.

"Did you notice the foot prints made by that Jason fellow when we were walking on the beach?"

"Not really," said Maxwell, "but I take it you did."

"Yes, and I'll bet money his would match those we saw at the cave entrance.

"But there were several of us up there," Maxwell said.

Lakefield thought about that, then remembered that Jason had stayed below and not joined them at the entrance.

"Maybe he climbed up to the cave before we got there this morning," said Maxwell, still not ready to believe anything suspicious. It just seemed too preposterous.

"I don't think so, but we can check with Coolridge and Helspath when we get back," Lakefield said.

"So," Maxwell said, getting a little more interested, "if those are his foot prints they've probably been erased by the others by now. What the heck was he doing there and when?"

"To get some gold or maybe to get a look see for his story before anyone else did. I don't know," said Lakefield. "We'll have a talk with Coolridge to see if Winslow was gone last evening or early this morning."

They finished putting up their tent, stored their supplies and put the body bag with the assumed remains of Dave Peterson in the tent. When they joined the others they were just in time to help Karen finish setting up the second tent.

"Thanks, Sheriff," Karen said. "If you're ready, let's get back."

They started walking back down the trail and Ben Maxwell tapped Lakefield on the shoulder to get his attention.

"As soon as we get back to Forks and you're sure about Peterson, I'll have to call his parents," Ben said.

Lakefield nodded and then quietly turned to Maxwell so the others couldn't hear.

"Yeah, I know," said Frank. "But say, Ben, I'd like you to lag behind a little on the way back and look at Winslow's shoe prints to see if you agree with me."

****

The Monrovia was heading south to Astoria, Oregon, where it would unload part of its wood chip cargo, pick up a load of dimensional lumber for the Japanese construction market and head for Osaka, Japan, and then Hong Kong.

The original plan was for Woo to stay with the ship. He would disembark in Hong Kong where Minister Wang had a scheme to get the "treasure" off the ship and into the People's Republic.

"What if the urn and gold coins are found but you can't get them back to this ship?" Varney had asked.

Woo told him that it would be his agents problem then. He and the agent with the search party could arrange to meet the ship in Oregon. If not, they would have to figure another way to get the treasure out of the country.

Now what? Thought Miles Varney. They had been forced to head south and the Coast Guard had followed them all the way to Ocean Shores. He had no idea of the fate of his two crewmen, Manoel and DeParmo and of the agent Woo. *Thank god I was paid in advance*, he thought. These Chinese were good employers, so the more he thought about it, the more he knew he had better try and contact them.

****

The weather in Beijing was unseasonably warm. Minister Wang Chin-tsi added to the heat under agent Lu's collar with another tirade.

"What do you mean he doesn't know where Woo is!" His face reddened.

"How about the urn and gold coins," he shouted.

Lu made a futile attempt to comment. "Minister, we don't know for sure that it ever ---------."

"Silence, you idiot. I know it may not have ever been there. It could have gone down with the ship or a thousand other possibilities, but saying we don't know anything!" Without taking a breath he went on.

Cave of Secrets

"What about agent Yang and his spy on the expedition?" the Minister asked.

"From what Varney's message said, he has not been able to contact Yang."

"All right," said a still irate Chin-tsi. "Let me know as soon as you hear anything else from Varney and if contact is made with Yang."

****

When Karen and the others left for the campsite on the bluff, the rest began the slow, meticulous work inside the cave. Chuck hadn't wanted to disturb the artifacts before he took some pictures, but temptation got the better of him and he and Bryan carefully started sifting through the debris.

The poor lighting and the dust made it difficult for Chuck to see. He was just about to clean his glasses when he spotted a piece of wood a few inches from where he was kneeling. Actually, it turned out there were three pieces.

"Bryan," Chuck said holding the wood pieces, "these look like parts of a small crate. See, you can almost make out some of the painted characters on this one."

Bryan knelt down beside Chuck.

"Yeah, I see, and the sheriff was right, someone, or several people have been in here very recently. The area has really been messed up and it looks like they moved several skeletons." Chuck thought to say that maybe the FBI warning hadn't been so far fetched, but Bryan had moved away and started digging. He soon found more wood pieces a few feet from where Chuck had found the others. However, these were larger and unpainted.

"Hand me one of those larger pieces over there, Bryan."

Chuck compared them. "The larger pieces are definitely plainer and more utilitarian than these with the painted sides."

"Let's take these outside in better light and then we'll ask Jerry to come in and run the detector around that spot by the larger wood pieces," Chuck said.

Jerry didn't need any coaxing. He was excited about going back in the cave.

Chuck yelled down to Bill and Will and told them to climb up and help Jerry.

"Try not to move too much until Karen gets here with the camera," Chuck told them as they passed him and climbed into the cave to join Jerry.

"Okay Bryan," said Chuck, "let's take a closer look at these wooden pieces." It felt good to be out in the fresh air.

The wood pieces were in amazingly good shape, probably because the cave had been sealed most of the last 1,500 years. Still, Chuck and Bryan took great care in examining each piece of wood.

Inside the cave, Bill and Jerry continued the conversation they had been having. Will listened with interest. He initially had been concerned about the skeletal remains. If they had been identified as native Indians, the cave would be considered sacred ground and he would have to demand they stop until he had talked to the Makah elders.

Chuck, Bryan and Frank Lakefield however had convinced Will that the remains were definitely non-Indian.

"Good God, Jerry," Bill said, "according to the sheriff, Dave was probably alive for quite a while after he got trapped inside. Must have caved in after him. Damn, why didn't he just wait for us that day?"

"We'll never know for sure." Jerry answered.

The detector Will was using registered strong readings. He waved his arms for the others to gather. They dug with their hands and the small trowels. Bill was the first to come up with a hand full of gold coins. "Wow!" he said.

Outside, Chuck and Bryan were trying to decipher the writing on the wood panel from the smaller crate.

"Look," said Chuck, "I think this refers to the Raja Suddhodana."

"Who was he?" asked Bryan. " I can't remember."

"He was the ruler of Sakya, a warrior who was elected from the Kshatriya class of the early Aryan society, somewhere about 500 BC. It is believed he was the father of the great Buddha Siddhartha Gautama."

Chuck continued his explanation. "To me, this proves the urn is here somewhere or at least was on that Chinese ship," said Chuck. Then Chuck studied the piece further.

"Here, look at this," he said, pointing to another character.

"Damn, this part is badly faded, but I think this character means mother. And this is a picture of a tree and a reference to Gaya."

"Yes, that is the Kai-skek character for mother," said Bryan.

"But where's Gaya?" he asked.

"Gaya was a region in what is now part of the State of Bihar in India."

"What are those symbols, Chuck?" said Bryan, pointing to some unfamiliar characters.

"This looks like a footprint, this is a wheel and here's that same tree again." Just then Chuck spotted the rest of the team returning.

Hal Burton

"Look, here comes Karen and the rest, let's put these pieces in that sack and we'll look them over again later. For now, I'm even more convinced of the existence of a ninth urn."

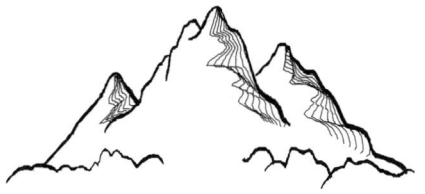

Chapter Fourteen

Chuck rose as Karen and the others neared. He greeted her with a hug.

"Here's the camera," Karen said, returning his embrace. Chuck gave her another squeeze and turned to Maxwell and Lakefield.

"And thanks to you two, also."

Then he turned to Jason.

"Okay, Jason, if you're ready let's get some pictures."

Just as Chuck started to yell up to Jerry and the others in the cave, Jerry stuck his head out and said that they had just found some gold coins.

"Okay Jerry," said Chuck, "but we've got to get in there and take some pictures before anything else is disturbed."

Chuck could tell by Jerry's body language that he was hesitant.

"Just give me a few minutes," Chuck said to Jerry. "I'm as excited as you are, but we need to get some pictures before everything gets messed up anymore." Jerry nodded and called inside to the others to bring out what coins they had found. They would take a break while Chuck photographed the scene.

Chuck and Jason climbed up and crawled inside.

"Really something, isn't it?" said Jason after they had taken several pictures.

Not getting any response, he turned to Chuck as he started to leave, "I would like to stay in here for awhile and take some more pictures. I can help out when the others return and start searching again."

Chuck couldn't see any reason why. "Okay, but ask Karen or Bryan or me before you touch anything." With that he stepped outside.

Jason was alone.

In no time Jerry and the rest would be back, so Jason figured looking for the urn was not feasible. While taking the pictures, he didn't see anything obvious that had been overlooked from the night before with Woo. He also sensed that Ben Maxwell and Frank Lakefield were taking more than a casual interest in him. This made him nervous. He knew he had to be careful.

But why, why me? he thought. *Had he said something to give himself away?*

Before he had a chance to do any searching by himself, he heard the others approaching the cave entrance.

By midday the searchers had found about a hundred coins, carefully removed what was left of the wooden chests, gathered what clothing and personal items of the Chinese that had not completely decayed and piled their skeletal remains in one corner of the cave.

"I count 15," said Bill.

"They must have been caught inside when a rock and mud slide sealed the entrance."

"Yes," said Karen. "Several of the skulls show signs of severe head wounds and many of the bones are broken, so some of them had to have been hit by large rocks during the slide."

"Chuck says we'll have to stay overnight," Jerry said, "but we should be done by noon tomorrow."

Jason listened while he searched in vain for any evidence of the urn, and assisted in the search for gold coins.

"Shouldn't we check in the hole where Jerry fell," Jason said.

"Good idea, Jason," said Bill.

Bill volunteered and with aid of a rope, carefully climbed down. As careful as he was, some more dirt broke loose and fell to the bottom.

"See anything?" said Jason.

"Not yet," said Bill. Nothing was found.

By three o'clock Bryan, with the help of Maxwell and Lakefield, had removed the skeletal remains from the cave. Everyone else continued the search.

"How many coins do we have now, Karen?" Maria asked.

"One hundred and thirty-two, and they're sure weird looking."

Each coin was round with a square hole in the middle. One side bore characters identified by Chuck to represent the Emperor of the Wei dynasty and a value symbol, also identified by Chuck, as the number five. The other side had the image of a dragon.

Chuck could not believe the coins were solid gold. That would have been very unusual. Most coins from the period were either 14 or 22 carat. These coins felt quite soft, so he figured they were 22 carat. They did register on the detectors, so they must have some alloy. Maybe silver. He speculated they must have been specially minted for the voyage of the monk Hwui Shan.

"What does the value five signify?" asked Maria, as she continued to search.

"Well around 200 BC a Queen Lu of the Han Dynasty issued what was then known as the Zhu coin," answered Bryan. That's spelled Z-H-U. Its value was a base value of one. Later, increasing trade demands called for higher denominations, so a 2, 3 and 4 Zhu coin was minted. Eventually, the Queen's Treasurer placed a 5 Zhu order, but I doubt they would normally have been made of gold. In this case, I'm really not sure what the value five denotes, but I still assume five Zhu."

"This is a significant find," Chuck said following up on Bryan's narrative.

"I know you're happy," Karen said to Chuck, "but remember, so far no urn."

"Yes, but we did find what I'm now sure are the sides of the chest that contained the urn," Chuck said. "So it must have been here at one time."

They also found several more pieces of the plain wood panels. Enough to reconstruct two large chests. The pieces were buried under silt next to where the coins were found.

Chuck told his crew to start gathering up all they have and get ready to head to the campsite in about 10 minutes. He left the cave and joined Maxwell and Lakefield. They talked about the possibilities of Jason Winslow being a conspirator in some scheme to steal some of the gold coins, or the more likely probability that he was just an overzealous reporter. Being overzealous, however, didn't explain the evidence that one or more people were either with him at the cave the previous night, or had been there about the same time.

Maxwell suggested that for now they try to bait Jason and see if he made any revealing mistakes, rather than directly confront him.

As the other team members approached from the hill, Chuck spoke loud enough for them to hear. "Sheriff, do you think we should leave someone here to guard the cave tonight?"

Continuing the ruse, Maxwell said, "There's no doubt someone was there last night."

They watched Jason's face for any reaction. If he was unnerved, he didn't show it. *Maybe we're wrong*, Chuck thought.

Jerry, unaware of their little act, said, "it should be okay, tonight."

Maybe that's for the best, thought Chuck. We can watch him to see if he tries to go back to the cave.

"All right, lets head back to the campsite," said Chuck. "We will not post a guard."

As they walked up the trail to the campsite on the bluff, it was almost sunset. Jerry caught up with Maxwell. "Can we talk about Dave Peterson and what you found?"

"Sure, but let's wait till we get to camp. We should have some time before dinner. Let's let Bill know, too."

****

"Here's what was left of Peterson's notebook," Maxwell said as he handed the fragile pieces of paper to Bill and Jerry.

"What a way to go," said Bill after reading what there was of the short note.

"Are you going to call the Peterson's?" asked Jerry, who had been reading along with Bill. "I'd like to talk to them."

"Yes. I think they are still in Portland, but I'll contact them either way. If you and Bill wish, I'll give you their number and you can call." Maxwell said.

****

Stan Granton looked over the registration list given to him by Jessica Lancaster. He had gotten the call early this morning, and after a briefing at the office in Olympia, he headed to Ocean Shores. Mrs. Lancaster at first seemed shocked when he presented his FBI identification, and more so, when he told her what he needed.

"So these are the only people who were checked in by Monday, and are still here?"

"Yes." She started to ask again what he was looking for, then stopped, as it had been obvious the first time, that he was not going to tell her. As a matter of fact, he wasn't so sure himself. The call to their regional office had come from a Commander Farnsworth of the Coast Guard. Stan had called Farnsworth back and gotten the gist of the story. In Stan's opinion, all he could do was check out the registration list and maybe, on some ruse, inspect the Gray Gull guestrooms of the ones who were still there. *But what was he looking for, anyway*, he thought.

****

John Yang was at wits' end. The Monrovia was headed toward Astoria Oregon without Woo. The plan would be to delay for two days. If Yang didn't show up in that time, the Monrovia would depart.

Yang still hadn't heard from Winslow. Any chance of finding the urn, stealing it away and meeting the ship before it left port was evaporating. He was about to go out for lunch when there was a knock at the door.

"Who is it please?" Yang asked.

"This is the manager, Mrs. Lancaster, and one of our maintenance men. We're doing an inspection of some of the rooms scheduled for remodeling. We'll only take a few minutes."

Yang kept the wireless radio in a second locked suitcase and took a quick glance to make sure all was put away. He hadn't wanted to raise any suspicions from the cleaning people.

"Sure, he answered, just a minute."

Opening the door, Yang was greeted by a woman he assumed was the manager and a younger man in coveralls.

"Yes, go ahead, I was just going to get something to eat and have a walk. Take your time," Yang said, unconcerned.

After Yang left, agent Granton, dressed in the coveralls of a motel maintenance person, did a quick, thorough search of the room. He noted the suitcases but made no move to open them. He could see nothing suspicious, but by now, he had pretty well concluded that about all the rooms they had inspected. He looked at the registration list.

"Mr. Yang is the last of the six guests still registered?"

She nodded.

"Has he indicated when he'll leave?" Lt. Mason asked.

"Sort of. He called to say he would be checking out today or tomorrow at the latest."

Hal Burton

"How many of the other guests we checked will be here till then?"

She thought for a minute. "I think at least one. But I'll look again, if it's that important."

"No, I guess that's it for now, Mrs. Lancaster. Thanks for your cooperation. If I need anything else, I'll call you. I'd like a copy of this list before I go."

****

"What did you say?" said Chuck, not hearing what Ben Maxwell had asked.

"Bryan, can you turn the sound down a little, please?" Maxwell said.

Ever since they had finished dinner, Bryan had been trying to pick up some news on his portable radio. Once they had left Rialto, he hadn't been able to bring in anything clear.

"What's so important tonight?" asked Jerry, mildly perturbed by the loud static.

"Just wanted to find out more about the Seahawks game this weekend." Bryan said. They play San Diego. I heard that Dan Fouts may not be able to start for them."

"Sorry, I'll try again later."

Maxwell thanked him and repeated the question to Chuck.

"What time do you plan to get started in the morning?" Maxwell asked.

"No later than 7 a.m.," he said. "We're about done, but I want to make sure all the coins have been recovered."

"What was the final count before we left?" Maxwell asked Coolridge.

"One hundred and thirty-nine."

Maxwell turned toward Lakefield. "Frank, let's you and I shoot to leave about 9:00. We'll go by the cave and then leave from there." Then, thinking for a moment, he turned back to Coolridge.

"Do you think you'll need us as security for the gold Chuck? After all, you've probably got over a million dollars worth."

Chuck hesitated, "Actually if you'd stay till we leave, I would feel a lot better."

"Okay," said Maxwell. "If it's okay with Frank, we'll leave when you do in the morning."

****

Nightfall came to the Olympic Peninsula. They gathered around the campfire. It burned bright and crackled with the cedar Jerry and Bill had gathered and added to the stack of kindling.

"This is the last night we'll all be together," said Chuck, "and I want to thank you for your help. Tomorrow I would like to leave by 10 o'clock. Frankly, we've found all that we can."

"Special thanks go to Ben Maxwell and Frank Lakefield for staying over tonight and for all the extra help today too," Chuck continued.

Everyone voiced agreement. Bryan even clapped a little.

Earlier in the day, Will had approached Chuck with a suggestion and Chuck thought it a good idea.

"Now, Will has asked to say something. Will."

"I know some of you need to get back right away, but this weekend is our annual Makah Days Celebration. I invite any and all to my home in Neah Bay for a cook out. Then we can go to the parade and fire works show. For anyone who wants to stay overnight, we have lots of room between my house and my mother's. I'd like very much to show you where I work and give you a tour of the Makah Center and Museum. It would be a great way to end our time together and celebrate."

"I think it's a great idea," said Maria. "Bryan, Karen, Chuck and I would have to drive all the way around through Aberdeen anyway, so why not stay in Neah Bay for the night and then go back the next day through Port Angeles. We can catch the ferry at Kingston."

"What about the gold?" said Bryan looking at Chuck.

"Yeah, you're right. I keep forgetting how much money we have," said Chuck.

Sheriff Maxwell turned to Chuck. "How about this," he said. "We'll be traveling as far as Forks with you anyway and when we get there you can put the coins in the vault at Seattle First National Bank."

He went on. "Then you can have the coins sent by armored car to wherever you want when you get back to Seattle. I would think you'd want to do something like that anyway, rather than transport everything back by yourselves."

"Great idea," said Chuck.

"I only wish we could come with you, it sounds like a good time," Maxwell said.

"Me too," said Jason. "But I need to get back and file my story."

"Bill, why don't you see if Kay can join us?" said Jerry.

"You can call her from Mora," said Karen.

So Maria, Bryan, Karen, Chuck, Jerry and Bill accepted the invitation. Frank and Ben would stay in Forks.

Several minutes passed and all of them seemed transfixed by the fire. As the fire slowly burned itself out, Chuck rose.

"Good night all, and thanks again for your help and friendship these past days."

Sounding more like a close friend than their leader, he concluded. "Let's hope we can wrap things up quickly tomorrow and be on our way. You've been a great team."

****

It was a beautiful morning and the sky over the ocean showed the promise of a clear, late summer day. In the distance a container ship could be seen moving north, likely heading for the Strait and then to Seattle. To the south two fishing boats were hauling in the first catch of the day.

Jason was frustrated. Even if he'd had a chance to slip away during the night, he only had his flashlight. Besides, he suspected he was being watched. The risks were too great. Could he sneak back later? Probably not. And the hole. Had it really been thoroughly checked out?

It was obvious also to Jason that Coolridge had about given up finding the urn. Yet, he still had that nagging feeling that they had missed something.

Jason helped the others gather everything together for departure.

****

Jerry, Chuck, Karen and Maria worked inside the cave. The rest, under Bryan's supervision, marked and packed all of the items found in the cave. The gold coins were placed in a special steel box that had been brought for that purpose.

Inside the cave, the team was getting frustrated.

"We've searched for an hour and only found one more coin," said Maria.

"Yes," said Karen. "And for sure, the urn is not here."

"Okay," said Chuck. "Let's give it another 30 minutes and we're on our way."

They all groaned.

"When we leave should we cover the cave opening?" asked Jerry.

"Sheriff Maxwell said we don't need to," answered Chuck, "but I don't feel good about it. I'm going to try and convince him to at least put some of that crime scene tape they use and wrap it around some of those large branches on the beach and lay them over the opening."

"Yeah, that would keep some people out, but it might also attract some that wouldn't normally have noticed the opening," said Jerry.

Chuck thought about that.

"Maybe if we're sure everything's out we should hire someone to permanently seal the cave," he said.

When about 40 minutes had passed and no more coins were found, Chuck said it was time to go. A few minutes later the group headed south down the beach. In the end, the sheriff left a sign at the cave entrance warning about the dangers of a slide. He planned to come back the following Tuesday anyway.

****

The hike from the Norwegian Memorial back to Rialto beach was harder than they had imagined. The sled that Sheriff Maxwell, Frank Lakefield and Bryan had fabricated to transport the bags with skeletons, the gold and the remains of Dave Peterson kept falling apart so they had to stop often for repairs. They hoped the skeletons of the Chinese crew would survive the trip and be in reasonably good shape to donate to the University of Washington Anthropology Department for further study.

About an hour later than Chuck had planned, they reached Rialto and the path to the Ranger station where they were parked. Once the vans were loaded, they said their good-byes to Jason.

"Bye the way, Jerry, what's the name of the ranger that's going to give me a lift back to Kalaloch?" Jason asked.

"Brad Ryan. He should be ready when you are, Jason," Jerry answered.

Jason turned to Chuck and the others.

"Thanks again for including me," Jason said.

"I'm heading back to Kalaloch and then Seattle as soon as I call my editor. Have fun this weekend in Neah Bay," he called, as he headed to Ranger Station and the pay phones.

Watching Jason walk away, Ben Maxwell turned to Lakefield and said, "Frank, I still don't know about that guy."

"I guess we'll never know for sure," Frank answered with a shrug.

Some more good-byes were said and then everyone went their own way. Most headed for Forks and Neah Bay. Jerry would follow in an hour after he talked to his boss, Craig Foster, and borrowed a car from the Mora station.

Hal Burton

Bill would head to Neah Bay, too, after he picked up his wife Kay in Forks. He called Kay and she was eager to see him and join the group in Neah Bay. Chuck's group would stop in Forks to put the gold coins in the bank, drop Bill off, and then head north.

Chapter Fifteen

August 1981

Several miles to the north, the archaeological students from Washington State University were dismantling their living quarters and the other buildings that supported the Ozette project. It was a shame to leave, but the site of the dig was now almost entirely reburied.

Until a few weeks ago, the dig had yielded artifacts over 1000 years old, but now the excavating was at an end, a victim of federal budget cuts. Many of the artifacts found were in the Makah Cultural Center in Neah Bay, but most of these would require hours of study before they could be positively dated and categorized. The source and date of some of the newly found artifacts belied explanation.

The project leader, Dr. David Cottie, had been visiting the site with some alumni in June when one of the students found a curious necklace. It appeared to be strung with bronze or copper coins. But that couldn't be, the Makah hadn't used money a 1000 years ago.

The Spanish and then the British explored the region in the 16th century and it was even speculated that Greeks had traded in the region before that. However, the markings on the coins looked Japanese or Chinese. If they were strung into a necklace, it didn't seem likely they were used for money, but rather for adornment.

The team from Washington State had talked about conducting further analysis of the necklace and the coins but by that time the project was terminated.

Like many of the other recent finds, it was tagged and readied for storage at Neah Bay. Hopefully, future study would be possible if federal money was restored.

As an afterthought, one of the students, Nel Adams, took a Polaroid picture of the necklace and put it in the file folder that went with the last shipment to the Center at Neah Bay. The folder was marked, "Ozette 1981, unknown necklace, likely 9th century."

****

There were only two pay phones at the Mora Ranger station. With all the weekend campers around, Jason had to wait several minutes. He really wanted to get this over with and head back to Seattle as soon as he could. Bill was using one phone to call his wife and some woman was on the other. Finally, it was his turn. After a few rings, Yang answered. Jason started to report, but Yang interrupted him with his news. He told Jason about the Coast Guard boarding of the Monrovia and the unknown whereabouts of Woo and the two crewmen. Jason couldn't believe that Woo was not on the ship. He told Yang of his and Woo's discoveries of the gold coins and the pottery shards. Then about how they had filled two bags with the coins. Finally, Jason told of the past two days at the cave.

"So, you saw Woo off, that night?"

Jason said yes and then told of his arrival back at the Coolridge team's campsite at Mora. He added that there had not been time to phone before they left for the cave.

"So, they didn't find the urn?"

"No, but sections of the wooden crate it may have been in were found. Which means the urn was there sometime and the pottery shards seem likely to confirm that."

"Perhaps," said Yang, "but if it was, it was taken by someone else years before or maybe completely destroyed and only the two pieces you found remained."

"How many coins did Coolridge find?"

"We found 140 coins. It is Coolridge's belief there are no more in the cave."

"So," Yang said, "you and Woo missed one hundred forty coins. If Woo was lost at sea or is in hiding, the rest of the coins are with him. Too bad that the urn was not found. Very well, I will advise Beijing."

Yang told Jason he would be checking out and that he would also contact the Monrovia when he got to his office. He didn't tell Jason that he might go to Astoria, if he heard from Woo. This seemed a remote possibility. The ship would leave tomorrow. He told Jason to return to Seattle, but that he would contact him the next day if need be.

Three hours later, John Yang was in his office and his message coded for transmittal.

****

Varney's message was given to Lu earlier, when it was late in the evening in Beijing. He knew of Woo's disappearance and had passed that information on to Minister Wang. He remembered the look on his face. Little was said. Now, early the next morning, he had been phoned and told there was a message from agent John Yang.

Yang's message had been decoded and given to Lu Xun.

"You're sure this is correct," he asked the communications technician.

"Yes, I've checked it twice," he answered with conviction.

"Very well," Lu said. "You may go."

He reread the message himself.

> 'Woo missing, urn not found. Coins found but with Woo.
> More Zhu coins found and secured by Coolridge.
> Monrovia in Port at Astoria for 1 more day.
> Await instructions.' - Yang

Lu placed the call to the Minister's office and was told that he would be back from a meeting at 3 o'clock.

Promptly at three Lu was shown into the Minister's office and without preamble, handed the message from Yang to Chin-tsi. After a moment he looked up at Lu.

"So, it is over and we have nothing to show for our effort."

Hesitantly, Lu responded, "Yes it would appear so Minister, unless Woo is alive and makes contact."

"And your agent Yang and his local agent?"

"They have returned to their normal duties for now, Lu answered, and I believe that we should advise Captain Varney to proceed on with his voyage. If Woo does make contact, and has the coins, we will have to devise another way to get the coins out of the U.S."

Minister Wang nodded approval.

"So the urn was either lost at sea or was never there. Is that what you're telling me?" looking intently at Lu.

"I believe so, Minister." He continued. "The only other possibility is that it was taken some time earlier. But when and by whom, I doubt we will ever know."

"You have done your best Lu. If there is a way for Yang or his agent to return to the area for another search we should try that. However it appears we have failed."

Lu left the Minister's office, wondering if this was truly the end of the story.

****

Jason Winslow wondered the same thing as he sat at the kitchen table in his small apartment on Capitol Hill in Seattle. He had only been back a few minutes and was having a snack before starting to write the article on the Coolridge expedition.

He had decided that he'd also write a short article on the finding of Dave Peterson's remains. If he could tie the two stories together it would make more interesting reading.

Jason had driven straight through from Kalaloch, eager to get back and away from the intrigue. It had felt good to be behind the wheel of his Datsun 280Z again.

He fingered one of the two Zhu coins he'd found and secreted away in his camera bag yesterday. *If you could only talk*, he thought. Of course, he could never show the coins to anyone, but the temptation had been too great not to keep a couple souvenirs. It's a wonder he hadn't been found out, anyway. Although nothing had ever been said, he felt that the sheriff, for one, was suspicious of him. Would the Sheriff talk to anyone about it? Would John Yang fall under any suspicion and involve him? He doubted it, but then determined that getting back to his regular job and getting a good story written and published about the expedition was the best thing he could do.

As he wrote his story, he couldn't get rid of a nagging feeling they had missed something in that cave. Coolridge was positive they had gotten all the coins. Jason knew that the previous night, Woo had found the two shards, which could be part of the urn or its top. Coolridge had taken all the pieces of wood presumed to be parts of the chests.

Working from the notes taken on the trip, he had a good first draft of the Coolridge treasure hunt story and the ties to ancient Chinese explorations.

He had decided to write two separate stories, and began the draft of the story about the end to the mystery of Dave Peterson's disappearance. Maybe his editor would see a way to tie the two together. He planned to take both stories into work on Tuesday, after the end of the three-day holiday. Thinking about it some more, he changed his mind and decided to go by the office on Labor Day.

Chapter Sixteen

The drive from Forks to Neah Bay was pleasant but tedious contending with the narrow and curving highway. Everyone was tired. Although no one said anything, it was a relief to be done with the search and everyone was looking forward to a fun night at Will's. The thought of sleeping in a real bed had its appeal. Karen and Maria both said that a hot shower would be wonderful.

As for Chuck, he was relieved to have the gold coins safely in the vault in Forks. He had held one out to examine more closely and to show Dean Ed Bailey next week. He had also brought along the wooden panels that he felt must have been the sides of the chest that once held the urn with the ashes of Buddha Gautama.

The Cultural Center and Museum was on the left just as they entered Neah Bay. Will was obviously excited to show them around and beamed like a first-time father when they assembled after parking the vans in the empty lot near the entrance.

"Come on," he called, "the Center's still open. I called ahead and they are waiting for us."

When they entered the Center, an attractive, middle-aged woman was sitting behind the reception counter. She rose to greet them.

"Hello, I'm Sarah and welcome to our Center." Will introduced Chuck, Karen, Bryan and Maria and explained that Jerry, Bill and his wife would probably get to Neah Bay later and would check here first before going to Will's house. If they missed them, they would still have a chance to visit the Center tomorrow.

"So, Sarah, you don't really have to stick around," Will said, "I can give them the tour."

"No, that's okay, I'd like to stay. Besides, I have something I want to ask Mr. Coolridge when you're done."

The museum portion of the Center contained many of the artifacts from the Ozette site as well as other examples of the Makah culture. A replica of a log house was constructed inside the building.

Will explained the exhibits. He was thrilled that Chuck and the team had come. Most exhibits had detailed signs, but Will seemed to enjoy his role so much, everyone went with the flow. They finished in about 45 minutes.

Will turned to Sarah, who had gone with them and occasionally offered a comment. "Okay, Sarah, it's your turn. You said you wanted to ask Chuck something."

"Thanks. A few days ago we got the last of the artifacts from the dig at Ozette. Without federal funds, we'll probably never get the help to correctly identify and date the recent finds."

"Anyway, one of the Washington State students took several Polaroid shots of some of the unidentified items and there's one I noticed of a necklace that looks to me like it has

Cave of Secrets

some Oriental writing on it. So I figured a Chinese expert like you might be able to tell me if it is Oriental."

She quickly added, "I doubt it though, because it's tagged as coming from a layer at the site dated approximately 1000 AD. I haven't had anyone look at the actual necklace yet, but saw the photo when I was filing everything this morning."

"Oriental writing? I doubt it too," said Chuck, "but let's see the photo. It's probably something more recent that was at one of the unburied locations and got mixed in with the artifacts from the dig when they were hurrying to finish up."

Sarah went back to the reception desk. She returned with a file folder and handed it to Chuck. "It's in here," she said.

Will, Bryan, Karen and Maria crowded around Chuck as he opened the file folder.

Karen broke the stunned silence. "My God, these are the same coins!"

"I know," Chuck said, pulling the coin from his pocket. He held it close to the picture.

Sarah Fairchild saw the coin in Chuck's hand and said, "How can this be?"

"Sarah, can we see the necklace?" Chuck asked.

"Follow me."

She led them back through the last part of the Museum tour path where there were staff offices and storage. Leaving them momentarily, Sarah went in one storage room and came out with a box marked, "Ozette, level 12, August 1981."

She opened the box, reached in and drew out the necklace.

"Wow," they all said in union. "Five Zhu coins," Chuck said.

There were 10 of the Zhu coins strung on what looked to be a leather thong. The thong was knotted on each side of each coin so they hung separately. The square holes in the center made it easy to string.

Chuck spoke first. "Sarah, as Will can tell you, we just put 139 of these same coins in the vault at Seattle First National in Forks." Then, holding out his hand to her, he went on. "Here's the 140th, and it's almost solid gold!"

"Solid gold," Sarah gasped. "Are you sure?"

"Yes, pretty sure, but you can have this one checked. I'm sure you'll find out it's real gold, probably 22 carat, and it will become a fascinating exhibit for your Museum."

Chuck and the others told her the story of the Chinese junk, the shipwreck in 500 AD, the cave and the mystery of the urn.

"How did this get to Ozette, I wonder?" Maria asked.

"We'll probably never know," Chuck answered, "but somehow these coins that were lost in 500 AD were uncovered in Ozette in a layer of earth dated around 1000 AD. The natives had no use for them as trade, so someone strung them into a necklace which ended up buried with everything else in the catastrophic slide."

"Could it be that the urn was at Ozette, too?" asked Bryan.

"It may well have been," said Chuck, dejected at the thought.

"If it was, it could have been destroyed and still buried," Karen said.

Then, Chuck added, "We'll never know, but I'd like to think it still exists somewhere."

"Sarah, thank you so much," Chuck said. "I'll send you a copy of my paper and a summary of our expedition, so you can have some background for what I'm sure will be one of your most interesting exhibits. Will, it's getting late. I think we should be getting to your place."

Will's place was on Cape Loop Road, just off the bay. He showed everyone around and asked Karen and Maria to get some things at the store for dinner while he got the barbecue grill fired up.

As Karen and Maria were leaving, Will's mom, Esther Grove, arrived from next door. Will paused to introduce everyone.

"Mom, you can show Chuck and Bryan where the card tables are and the extra chairs, while I get this grill going," Will said.

"Sure Willis, where's Bill and Jerry?"

"Bill's picking up Kay and Jerry had to check with his boss and borrow a car from the Mora station," he answered. "They should all be here by dinner."

****

Karen and Maria walked to the store following Will's directions. Karen decided to break the ice and ask Maria about Jerry.

"I know you and Jerry hit it off on this trip. Do you have any idea where it's going to go from here?"

Maria hesitated for a minute and then shrugged.

"We really like each other, but we haven't quite faced the issue of the distance between us. My god, he's at Kalaloch and I'm in Seattle!" she said. My classes start in two weeks, too. This weekend up here will give us time to discuss things, I hope."

"How about you and Chuck?"

"I think we'll get officially engaged and married next year," Karen said.

"He hasn't directly popped the question, but I think he intends to after this next quarter and when he finishes his Ph.D."

They walked on in silence for the next block.

"Oh, look, there's the store Will told us about," Maria said.

Maria and Karen finished shopping and got back to Will's just as Bill and Kay arrived. Jerry was still not there.

"Everybody, this is my wife Kay, who most of you know is also Jerry's sister," Bill told them proudly.

Esther Grove stepped forward, "Hi, Kay, we met before once, when Willis and Bill went hiking."

"Yes, I remember, thanks for having us." Turning to Chuck, "And thanks for including me in your celebration party. I've missed Bill and it sounds like you all had an exciting time," Kay said with a smile.

"Well, this was Will's idea, so thanks go to him," Chuck said, "but you're welcome anyway. Bill was a lot of help and we really appreciated him joining us."

Just then, Jerry arrived and after saying hello to Mrs. Grove, he went over to Maria and gave her a hug.

"Guess what we saw earlier at the Museum," Maria said to Jerry.

"Yeah," said Will, "You'll never guess." Jerry looked at Maria, Will and Bryan and then at Chuck.

"Okay, I give up."

"I'd like to know, too," said Esther Grove. "Because whatever it was it sure got you all fired up," she laughed.

Chuck cleared his throat to get their attention. "Bill, Jerry, we saw a necklace strung with Zhu coins. Identical to the ones we found in the cave."

"How could that be?" Bill and Jerry asked together.

****

"That was a great meal," said Bryan. Everyone agreed.

"Thanks to Will and especially Mrs. Grove," said Chuck turning to Will's mother.

"Now Will, I think its time for another of your great tales. Maybe even a look at that strange totem of yours," Chuck went on. "We may never solve the mystery of the coin necklace, but maybe we can help Will solve the riddle of his strange totem."

"Yes," they all chimed in. "It would make a fitting end to our adventure. After all, we now have your mother here to tell us the real story." They all laughed.

"Okay, you win, but if Mom doesn't mind, I'd rather we go next door to her house and then I can show you the totem and some of the other Makah relics we have at the same time," Will said.

"Sure, that's fine," his mom answered, "but first you all clean up here and give me a few minutes to straighten up next door. And Will, before it gets too late, you need to figure out the sleeping arrangements. I have room for four next door."

****

As the group in Neah Bay was getting ready to go next door to Will's Mom's home, Jason Winslow dropped his stories off at the office. He left them in his editor's in-basket with a note that he would be in Tuesday morning. It was close to dark now and he turned on his headlights as he pulled out of the parking lot on Broad Street and headed back to his apartment

The phone was ringing as he entered.

"Jason, this is John Yang."

Yang had never contacted him at his home. He would call at work and then they would meet at a prearranged spot.

"I'm calling from the pay phone across the street. Meet me in five minutes at the corner. I'm driving a blue Ford sedan."

Once in the car, Yang took no time in bringing Jason up to date. There had been no contact from Woo and the Monrovia was leaving Astoria in the morning. His superiors in Beijing wanted one more search of the cave. Jason started to comment, but Yang continued. When Yang was done, Jason said nothing at first.

Then, incredulously, "You want me to go back and search the cave? Coolridge was certain there was nothing left to be found. Maybe we did miss some coins, but everyone agreed that the urn was gone."

"That may be," said Yang, "but if there's any way you can return tomorrow and have a final look, then I can assure Beijing that we have done everything possible."

"But what if I'm seen, or the authorities have returned?"

"Just say you needed a few more details for your story."

As hard as he reasoned with Yang, he could not change his mind. In the morning he would once again take I-5 south, pick up HWY 101 and head back to the ocean by himself.

****

The same evening Jason planned his return, FBI Special Agent Steve Collins was working late at his office in Seattle.

He was waiting for a phone call from Stan Granton in Olympia. Earlier that day Collins was reviewing Granton's report and saw the name John Yang. Could this be John Yang the Taiwanese Consul? The John Yang that still, occasionally, fed him sensitive information? Probably not. The phone rang.

"Stan, thanks for calling so late."

After Granton's description, Collins was convinced that it was the same John Yang. He thanked Granton and feigned off any questions as to his particular interest.

The Coast Guard had been convinced that either Yang or one of 3 or 4 others registered at the Grey Gull had been communicating with a Liberian registered ship. Granton had seen nothing suspicious to warrant further investigation and sent his report in to Seattle.

Collins thought, *Why was the Taiwanese Consul staying at the Grey Gull? Why not!*

The Liberian ship had been inspected and nothing of suspicion found. The messages to the ship had been in some type of code. Yet, there was no proof that Yang was the sender of the messages. Collins decided that he personally would call Commander Farnsworth of the Coast Guard. There was really nothing to be done, but thank him for his diligence. When he next saw John Yang, he would ask him what he did for Labor Day weekend. *Speaking of Labor Day weekend*, he thought. It was time for him to go home. The traffic on the Lake Washington floating bridge was lighter than usual and he found his thoughts returning to John Yang, the Coast Guard report and Granton's investigation. The report from Washington DC about the Chinese spy also nagged at his conscious. Perhaps he should keep a closer eye on Mr. Yang.

****

Mrs. Grove's home was similar to her son Will's but furnished with a feminine touch and as Will had told them, decorated almost exclusively with Native American pictures, pottery and wall hangings. Downstairs was the kitchen, living room, a study, two large bedrooms and a full bathroom. Upstairs was her bedroom, bathroom and a storage room. Off the living room was an enclosed porch with a beautiful view of the bay.

"The porch has a couch with a hide-a-bed, so with the two downstairs bedrooms we can accommodate several of you," she said.

She turned to Will. "Why don't you see who wants coffee and then you can get started. And Will, I moved the totem into the study."

When everyone was seated and had coffee, Will excused himself. Shortly, he returned with the totem.

"It sure is different," said Jerry. "Pretty much like you described."

Bryan went over to Will and took a closer look. "Actually," Bryan said, "this three-eyed face is weird. It almost appears oriental. And see this, the two outside eyes are definitely Mongolian, and look at the large ears."

"Didn't someone say earlier that it could be an alien," laughed Karen.

"You know," said Chuck," the center eye is really different, almost like a large dot."

"You're right," said Bryan. "I think you've hit on an idea."

"Look," he continued pointing to the face. "If you move the middle, smaller one slightly higher and assume an Oriental look, what do you have?"

"The face of a Buddha!" said Chuck. "You're right."

"I don't understand," said Jerry.

Bryan explained. "On statues or pictures of the Buddha, a dot on the forehead is symbolic of a third eye which indicates that the Buddha sees all." He went on.

"The long ears indicate that he hears all. And look here. See the forehead protrudes slightly indicating a large brain. That signifies to believers that he knows all."

"Will," said Chuck, "you already told us that this Totem was definitely not carved in recent times. Are you sure?"

"You know there were lots of Chinese immigrants around Port Angeles and the Buddha image may have come from some involvement with them."

"No, I'm sure this predates that," said Will. Then, turning to Mrs. Grove. "Isn't that right, Mom?"

"That's for sure," said Mrs. Grove. "It's at least 400 to 500 hundred years old because I've seen rock carvings that look similar, and those were very old."

"That's right," said Bryan, "Will and I did talk about the petroglyphs, but I thought that was the fifth image not this one with the face."

"It was," said Will, "but I forgot about Mom also seeing that petroglyph of a face several years ago."

Esther Grove nodded and then glanced at her watch. "I'm sorry, Will, I almost forgot about my senior's meeting at the Center. I'm going to have to leave for a while, but I should be back before you all go to bed."

"Sorry you have to leave now," said Karen. Everyone else agreed and thanked her again for her hospitality. After she left, Will turned to Bryan.

"So what about this fifth carving?" Will asked.

"I don't know," said Bryan taking another close look at the totem.

"You know," said Maria pointing to the four upright parts protruding from the four square layers, "we've called these things flags or feathers, but could they represent sails?"

"My God," said Chuck. "You are right. They could be. But for what purpose? This certainly doesn't look like a ship."

"Any sailors in your family tree, Will?" said Jerry with a chuckle.

"None that I know of. Thanks for your ideas but I'm as mystified as the rest of you. Anyway, why don't I go ahead and tell you about some of the other things mom has here before it gets too late. I'll ask her in private some time about any sailors on leave."

Chuck and the group listened to Will's story of the rest of the Makah items in his mom's living room, but as he listened Chuck had that feeling that the answer to the origin of the strange carvings on the totem was a story within itself.

When Will finished his talk the group split up and said their goodnights. Bill, Kay, Chuck and Karen stayed at Mrs. Grove's. Jerry, Maria and Bryan went with Will to his home.

Nighttime settled in on the small community of Neah Bay. Tomorrow the team would say goodbye and their adventure would be over.

Chapter Seventeen

Jason was irritated with himself when he realized he had overslept and it was already past 8 o'clock in the morning. He wanted to leave by 9 to beat the holiday traffic. After a quick shave and shower he dressed and deciding to eat on the way, heading for the door. Just then the phone rang. He hesitated and then decided to answer.

"Hello." It was his editor, Jake Swanson.

"Jason, good morning."

"Mr. Swanson," said Jason, puzzled about the call. "Good morning."

"You're probably wondering why I'm calling you at home on the weekend, but I came into the office today to check on some stories for tomorrow's edition and found your articles in my basket," he said. "Fascinating, fascinating! I think the story on Peterson should run as a sidebar to the Coolridge story. "What do you think?"

Jason was flabbergasted. Swanson had never been this enthusiastic about his work before.

"I think that's great, Mr. Swanson," Jason said. "Thanks."

"Well then if you have no objection, I'll do a little editing and we'll plan these for Tuesday's paper. Should make good human interest stories for the week after Labor Day."

Jason was tempted to tell Swanson about his plan to go to the ocean cave site today, but how would he explain his reasons?

"Are you going to be around in case I have any questions?" Swanson asked.

Hesitating, Jason said, "I'm going to be gone all day today, but if you like, I can come in tomorrow."

"That will be great, and Jason, good job," Swanson said.

Jason sat for a minute and thought to himself, *After all this time, finally I get some of the recognition I deserve.* Then out loud, "Maybe I shouldn't go to the ocean." But he knew that he must go if only to satisfy his own need for closure and get Yang to give him some respect if he found what no one else could.

****

The highways were packed with cars loaded with families all madly trying to get somewhere for this last weekend of summer. Jason didn't get to Rialto Beach until much later than he had hoped. He got one of the last parking spaces. There was still plenty of daylight and, fortunately, the tide was on the way out.

He was a little nervous that someone he knew, like Jerry Helspath, might still be around, but then he remembered they were all up at Neah Bay, at Will's place for some kind of Makah celebration. Jason had stopped in Olympia at a 7-Eleven and grabbed some sandwiches.

He placed the sandwiches in his backpack along with his flashlight and some other gear and set out for the cave. It was overcast and he thought he felt a light sprinkle as he made his way north. There were several other hikers on the beach.

"Nice day," one of them said as Jason passed him.

Jason grunted and nodded and quickly moved ahead toward Cape Johnson.

****

Break-ins and occasional car thefts were quite unusual at the more public campsites and trailheads in the Olympics, but they did occur. More often cars were burglarized at the remote trailheads. This Labor Day weekend, however, a gang of car thieves was working the parking lots along the coast.

Jason hadn't seen the young man watching him as he left his car and headed toward the beach and the trail north. When Jason was well out of sight, the man approached Jason's Datsun 280-Z and in a matter of seconds had the window down and the door open. Datsun's were a popular car and high on the list of "most stolen."

With a few quick wire connections under the dash the car started up. Almost as quickly, the man drove it out of the lot and headed in the direction of Highway 101.

****

The closer Jason got to the cave the more excited he got. Hopefully, no one would be around so he could safely climb into the entrance without being seen. Otherwise, he'd likely have to explain what he was doing there, especially with the warning signs the sheriff had posted at the entrance. He figured he would only stay an hour or so. If, after that, he still hadn't found anymore traces of the urn, he would leave with enough time to get back before high tide. It was starting to rain, so he quickened his pace.

Luckily, there was no one around when he got near the Memorial. He quickly headed toward the now familiar cliff and climbed up the bank. In a matter of seconds, he was sliding around the warning signs, and crawling into the cave. As far as he could tell, no one had seen him.

His flashlight wasn't much help, so he lit two of the candles he had brought and began his search, concentrating on the area where he remembered the small chest parts had been found. He also planned to search in the hole where Jerry had fallen.

Time seemed to go by quickly. He glanced at his watch. Better hurry, he thought.

Outside, it was raining harder and he heard thunder in the distance. Nevertheless, he focused on the search. After another half-hour Jason had found nothing except a bone which he figured was overlooked when they packed up the skeletons.

Then he carefully climbed down into the hole. He dug around using the light from his flashlight. He had just about given up when he found a small shard of pottery. He examined it closely in the beam of his flashlight. Probably another piece of the urn top, he thought. *Maybe it is still here!* The find excited him and he continued to dig around in the dirt.

There was another crack of thunder that sounded closer and then a flash of lightning. He knew he should leave but continued digging. There was another loud thunderclap and the whole cave seemed to shudder. Definitely time to leave he thought. Just then a flash of lightning lit up the whole cave and, to Jason's horror, dirt and rocks started falling down around him. A deafening clap of thunder reverberated in the cave.

"My God," he screamed.

The candles that he had burning above blew out and he could no longer see light overhead. He crawled out of the hole just as another loud thunderclap sounded. More dirt fell. Then it was silent. Using his flashlight to guide him he dug frantically where the entrance once had been. After a few minutes he had made no progress and was exhausted from his efforts. It was getting harder to breath. He rested a while and then started digging again in desperation. The flashlight started to dim.

****

"Good morning Mr. Sleepyhead," Kay said to Bill, poking him lightly. "Rise and shine, Mrs. Grove's up already and she and I have pancakes about ready." Bill didn't move.

"Karen and Chuck are up too and she's gone next door to invite the rest over for breakfast."

"All right, all right, I'm awake," said Bill, rubbing his eyes. Then he reached for her. "Now behave yourself!" Kay said, realizing it had been almost a week since they had been together.

"Okay," groaned the rejected suitor. "What time's that parade today?"

"Mrs. Grove said it starts at 11 o'clock," she answered, giving him a kiss on the forehead. As he dressed, she told him of her conversation with Karen that morning about Jerry and Maria.

"So, it's pretty serious for those two," he said.

"Sure sounds like it from what Maria told Karen."

"That's great. Maybe you'll have a sister-in-law after all."

Next door at Will's house the rest of the group was up and getting ready to go to Mrs. Grove's. Bryan and Jerry had bunked together in one room. Maria had a room to herself. Jerry had had other ideas, but Maria said no. Chuck and Karen had split up too, in deference to Mrs. Grove.

After finishing a great breakfast they had about an hour before the parade started.

"How about if we go to the museum now, Will?" Jerry asked.

"Yeah, that's a good idea," Will answered. "Why don't you go next door and see if Bill and Kay are ready and I'll meet you over there in about 10 minutes."

"Chuck," Will hollered toward the living room. "Do you want to go with us to the Center?"

Chuck thought a moment but decided he had too much to do today to get ready to leave.

"No, no thanks. I'll pass this time."

Chuck really wanted to get back home, as did Bill and Jerry, but Will wanted them to see the parade and Jerry and Bill wanted to see the necklace. So with the understanding that they would leave after the parade was over, each busied themselves with organizing and packing for the day's trip.

"All right Chuck, I'm leaving to get the others," said Will as he closed the door and headed to his mother's.

"Okay," said Chuck, "and remember, I'd like us to all meet back here after the parade."

Then Chuck went to find Bryan. He found him in the kitchen having another cup of coffee with Karen.

"About done packing Bryan?" he asked.

"Yes, just a few last minute things when we get back after the parade."

"How about the notes for our meeting with the dean?" Chuck asked. Chuck had told Bryan that on Tuesday they would meet with Dean Bailey, compare notes, and prepare a complete review of their trip and discoveries.

"Yes, I'm about done there too, but I do have a question, Chuck."

Bryan went right on without waiting for an answer.

"What about all the skeletons in those bags in the van?"

"We can check with the dean, but I think we should turn them over to the Anthropology Department for analysis. I don't know what to do with them after that."

"How about the coins when we get them from the bank in Forks?"

Chuck thought for a moment. "They should be given to the university, but with Dean Bailey's approval, I'd like to give one coin to each member of our team, even that pest Jason," Chuck said. "It would be a nice souvenir and reminder of the good times we had together."

****

When Jerry returned from the Center and Museum, he found Maria out on the porch sitting in the swing.

"Can I join you?" he asked, but she'd already moved over when she saw him. He sat down and took her hand.

"Wasn't that something," she said.

"If you mean the necklace, yes. What a coincidence and it sure adds to the mystery," Jerry said. "Still, it doesn't answer the questions about the missing urn, does it?"

She nodded and then sensed that Jerry was thinking about something else. He gently squeezed her hand.

"Listen Maria," said Jerry, "I think I'm falling in love with you. I know it's going to be difficult seeing each other with the distance and all, but I don't want to lose you."

"Me neither," she said moving closer and holding his hand tighter.

"So," he said, "I called Mr. Foster before you got up this morning and I talked to him about transferring."

"He mentioned there just happened to be an opening in October at the Snoqualmie Station. That's only about an hour away, isn't it?"

"Yes, about an hour. By the way, I think I love you too."

****

They were all glad they had stayed for the parade. It was great fun. Afterwards, they met in Mrs. Grove's living room.

"Thanks for coming back. I know we're all eager to get home," Chuck said.

"First, I want to tell you that I just finished talking to Sheriff Maxwell and he told me that there was a good sized slide at our cave site yesterday and it completely covered the entrance. He got a call from three hikers who were near the

Memorial when a thunder storm rolled in and were trying to get under the rock overhang to stay dry when they realized the hillside was giving way. They just got out of the way in time."

"Anyway, they're okay and Maxwell says the slide solved the problem of someone getting hurt in the future. He's going back over there today to check on everything. Interesting, too, he has another mystery to unravel. Seems the same hikers found a body washed ashore about two miles north of the Memorial. No identification yet, but the lifejacket the man had on was from a ship the SS Monrovia."

"Finally, I want to thank Will and Mrs. Grove again for their hospitality and all of you for your great effort. Will, I know your Mom's still in town, so please pass on our thanks."

Turning back to the group. "We didn't find the urn, but from what Bryan and I have seen, it was in the cave at one time. We did find a lot of the gold coins and I believe enough evidence to conclude that a Chinese junk did shipwreck on our coast almost 1,500 hundred years ago."

"The ancient records about the great Buddha say there were eight urns containing his ashes. These were supposedly buried after his death in 483 BC, as I've told you. So whether the urn we think was in the cave was one of those or a ninth one, I guess we'll never know."

"Good luck and I hope we'll all keep in touch," Chuck finished. "It's been a great adventure and certainly a lot of fun being with you."

Chapter Eighteen

Esther Grove was sorry to see Willis' friends leave. They had had a good time. It had been quite a festival and she was glad that Willis was home and here to enjoy it with her. She spent the rest of the day watching the parade and visiting with friends at the Senior Center. When she got back, everyone was gone. She thought about going next door, but didn't.

After eating dinner alone, she was tired and ready for sleep. She climbed the stairs to her bedroom mindful of the emptiness the house had since Willis' father had left her. For a minute, she glanced out the window at the bay where the last of the sun's rays gave the ships in the harbor a rusty orange color. How beautiful, she thought. As darkness came, she turned on the lamp at her bedside. *I should have shown them this lamp*, she thought.

Willis' father had made the lamp for her only a few months before he died and it always reminded her of his love and kindness. It was such a beautiful lamp and she had been very happy when her husband had suggested making it from the old vase that had been in her family for years.

No one really knew how long, but Esther remembered seeing it in her grandfather's storage room when she was a little girl. This shade's too big, she thought. It obscures the beauty of the vase. She tilted the shade back to get a better view.

Its' primary color was a deep blue, almost purple and the sides had patterns of colorful footprints, wheels and strange looking trees painted in bright greens and red browns.

Her grandfather used to say that the vase was very old and mystical. If you put it to your ear you could hear the sounds of the ocean and the voice of our ancestor who came from the sea many ages ago.

Hal Burton

Norwegian Memorial

魏Epilogue

Fall 1982

Chuck Coolridge received his Ph.D. in June and his dissertation on Ancient Chinese Explorations was published in several periodicals including the alumni magazine, *Columns*.

Karen Black and Chuck Coolridge got engaged in July. She continues to teach history at Samamish High School in Bellevue, Washington.

Jerry Helspath and Maria Lee were married in May and settled in their home in North Bend Washington. Bill Jenkins was his best man.

Willis Grove works part time as a Makah Ranger at the Ozette site and continues working at the Cultural Center in Neah Bay. He, Bryan Hill and Chuck Coolridge were Ushers at Jerry and Maria's wedding.

Captain Miles Varney sold his interest in the ship Monrovia after a dispute over the loss of two crewmen. One washed ashore near the Norwegian Memorial, the other was never found.

The mystery of Jason Winslow's disappearance is still unsolved. Foul play is suspected because his car was found stripped and abandoned in a parking lot in Portland, Oregon. Jason's two stories with his byline were published the Sunday after Labor Day in 1981.